Danger
—on the—
Flying Trapeze

Trailblazer Books

TITLE	HISTORIC CHARACTERS
Abandoned on the Wild Frontier	Peter Cartwright
Attack in the Rye Grass	Marcus & Narcissa Whitman
The Bandit of Ashley Downs	George Müller
The Betrayer's Fortune	Menno Simons
The Chimney Sweep's Ransom	John Wesley
Danger on the Flying Trapeze	Dwight L. Moody
Escape from the Slave Traders	David Livingstone
Flight of the Fugitives	Gladys Aylward
The Hidden Jewel	Amy Carmichael
Imprisoned in the Golden City	Adoniram and Ann Judson
Kidnapped by River Rats	William & Catherine Booth
Listen for the Whippoorwill	Harriet Tubman
The Queen's Smuggler	William Tyndale
Quest for the Lost Prince	Samuel Morris
The Runaway's Revenge	John Newton
Shanghaied to China	Hudson Taylor
Spy for the Night Riders	Martin Luther
The Thieves of Tyburn Square	Elizabeth Fry
Trial by Poison	Mary Slessor
The Warrior's Challenge	David Zeisberger

Danger
—on the—
Flying Trapeze

DAVE & NETA JACKSON
Text Illustrations by
Julian Jackson

BETHANY HOUSE PUBLISHERS
MINNEAPOLIS, MINNESOTA 55438

Published by Bethany House Publishers
A Ministry of Bethany Fellowship, Inc.
11300 Hampshire Avenue South
Minneapolis, Minnesota 55438

Printed in the United States of America

Library of Congress Cataloging-in-Publication Data

Jackson, Dave
    Danger on the flying trapeze / Dave and Neta Jackson ; text
illustrations by Julian Jackson.
        p.   cm. — (Trailblazer books ; 15)
    Summary: When he and his mother join the Fourpaugh Circus in
1893, fourteen-year-old Casey Watkins is certain that their lives will
change for the better, but the real change comes when they meet the
charismatic evangelist D. L. Moody.
    [1. Moody, Dwight Lyman, 1837–1899—Juvenile fiction. 2. Moody,
Dwight Lyman, 1837–1899—Fiction. 3. Circus—Fiction. 4. Christian
life—Fiction,] I. Jackson, Neta. II. Jackson, Julian, ill. III. Title.
IV. Series.
PZ7.J132418Dan   1995
[Fic]—dc20   95–10048
ISBN 1–55661–469–1   CIP
                                                            AC

Forepaugh's Circus was booked for two weeks at the Chicago World's Fair (the World's Columbian Exposition) in 1893, from June 5 through June 18. For this story, however, we have cut the time the circus was in Chicago to nine days, including the two Sundays (June 11 and June 18) when Dwight L. Moody rented the circus tent.

The major circus characters—Joe McCaddon, the Eugene Brothers trapeze act, Eph Thompson, Addie Forepaugh, Jr., and his wife, Lillie Deacon—were all real people and part of Forepaugh's Circus at various times in the late 1880s through the early 1890s. Our research could not determine, however, which acts were still part of the circus in 1893. We borrowed the "John L. Sullivan" boxing elephant act, developed by Eph Thompson and taken over by Addie Forepaugh, Jr., from Forepaugh's circus program of 1885.

Casey Watkins and his family are entirely fictional, although he is the sort of young person Dwight L. Moody often befriended and helped send to one of the two schools he founded in Massachusetts.

DAVE AND NETA JACKSON are a husband/wife writing team who have authored or coauthored many books on marriage and family, the church, and relationships, including the books accompanying the Secret Adventures video series, the Pet Parables series, and the Caring Parent series.

They have three children: Julian, the illustrator for the Trailblazer series, Rachel, a college student, and Samantha, their Cambodian foster daughter. They make their home in Evanston, Illinois, where they are active members of Reba Place Church.

CONTENTS

Chapter 1

Skipping School

CASEY WATKINS JAMMED his cold hands into the pockets of his thin jacket, hunched his back against the biting February wind, and angrily aimed a kick at a tin can that lay in his path. "I *hate* Philadelphia!" he growled to himself as the can bounced loudly off the brick wall of a factory.

He was walking beside a railroad siding where unused train cars were parked, going nowhere in particular—just anywhere the truant officer couldn't find him. Avoiding the truant officer, whose job it was to catch kids who skipped school, had been happening more and more lately. Now, trudging through the dirty snow between the railroad tracks and the backs of the ugly, squat factories, Casey knew he'd be in trouble when Mama found out that he had ditched school again. But he couldn't stand it! Ever since they'd had to sell the farm and move to the city four months ago, the boys at school had been making fun of his red hair, calling him "dirty Irish mick," pushing him for no reason just to see if he'd get mad. Even worse were the girls who giggled behind their hands when he stumbled over a word in reading.

"Don't know why I have to go to school anyway," Casey mumbled bitterly. "I'm fourteen now—almost a man. Should be workin' to support Mama and Cara since Papa died. But no. Uncle John says I have to go to school—"

The boy stopped short and stared. There, sitting on top of a flatbed car on a railroad siding, was the strangest contraption he'd ever seen. The bottom looked like some sort of cart or wagon and was painted a glittery gold that sparkled in the winter sunshine. But the top was carved into the shape of a medieval knight locked in combat with a large, green, slithery dragon.

Startled, Casey stared at the strange wagon. Then, looking around, he realized it was just one of many unusual railroad cars parked on the siding. Fancy parade wagons and large animal cages were chained to several flatbed cars. Others resembled regular passenger cars and boxcars—the kind that hauled livestock or equipment—except they were painted bright colors and each car loudly proclaimed along its side in bold, fancy lettering:

Forgetting all about school and the truant officer and Uncle John, Casey broke into a trot, which brought him closer to two enormous buildings with colorful flags fluttering from each corner. Pasted all over the backs and sides of the buildings were large posters showing giant elephants, prancing horses, clowns, midgets, acrobats, beautiful girls, and the words, "Greatest Show on Earth . . . Adam Forepaugh Circus!"

Casey was excited and confused at the same time. He'd never seen a circus before, but he'd heard about the gypsylike caravans that traveled from town to town, where daredevil performers and trained animals did amazing tricks under a great big canvas tent. But what did that have to do with these strange railroad cars and huge buildings?

A sign hung over the enormous doors on the back of one of the buildings. "Winter Quarters, Forepaugh Circus," Casey read slowly. So that's what this was!

Just then the big double doors swung open and a

large, gray elephant lumbered out. Heart thumping, Casey flattened himself against the building as the huge creature plodded past.

"Hey, kid!" yelled the black man who was leading the elephant with what looked to Casey like a very small chain. "Outta the way . . . don't want ya ta get hurt!" And then the pair plodded on through the muddy slush along the railroad siding, looking for all the world like a man taking a giant dog for a walk.

The huge double doors were still standing open. Curious, Casey peered inside. The warm, pungent odors of straw, hay, and manure assaulted his nose . . . just like they used to in his father's horse barn. Animal stalls and pens stretched as far as he could see. Spying a bucket half full of water sitting near the door, Casey grabbed it and walked down the long corridor of stalls, trying to look as if he belonged there.

The big, barnlike building seemed both familiar and, at the same time, like a different world. The first set of stalls were occupied by hefty workhorses— not like the trim racehorses his father, Jack Watkins, used to breed and train. He passed a blacksmith with bulging muscles, who was trimming the massive hoof of one horse, two midgets who were busy mending harnesses, and a woman with long, waist-length hair who was tinkering with an odd-looking bicycle. The whole place was buzzing with activity. A few people glanced at him curiously, but most were busy yelling to someone else, feeding animals, or mucking out animal pens.

With the water bucket as his passport, Casey

continued walking down the long corridor of stalls, past horses and ponies of all descriptions, as well as piles of ropes, pulleys, and bales of straw. As he turned a corner, he saw another long corridor, but this one contained rows of cages. He squinted into the dim light and saw tigers pacing back and forth, a hippopotamus, monkeys, bears, and . . . he couldn't see any farther. He desperately wanted to look, but a man in riding boots who was carrying a short, leather whip was talking loudly with a woman near the cages, so Casey hurried on.

On the other side of the building was a whole row of matching white horses with long, silky manes and tails. *Wow,* Casey thought, *wouldn't Mama love to see these beauties!* He remembered Mama galloping across the lush pasture of their horse farm, her rusty red hair flying in the wind, laughing gaily as Papa tried to catch her on another horse. Then he winced as he thought of his pretty mother now, stuck in their small, ugly apartment, hunched over the sewing Aunt Mary collected from women in Uncle John's parish.

Casey had come almost the full way around the building when he saw the elephants. The big beasts stood docilely side by side, each with a short chain around its leg fastened to a big metal stake pounded into the ground. *One, two, three* . . . he counted breathlessly . . . *eight, nine, ten.* He never expected to see one elephant in his life, much less ten!

"Hey! You with the bucket!" a familiar voice yelled. Casey jumped. He'd forgotten about the man he'd run into outside. For a split second he was tempted to run, but the man and elephant number eleven stood between him and the doors.

Casey swallowed. "Yes, sir?" he managed.

The black man looked him up and down. "You got something in mind for that bucket of water?"

Casey turned red. "N-no, sir."

A grin spread across the man's face. "Then how 'bout giving Queen Victoria here a drink."

Uncertain what he should do, Casey took a few steps toward the elephant and set the bucket down. The long trunk snaked forward and plopped into the bucket. Sucking up a quarter of the water, the elephant then swung the end of her trunk back into her mouth and squirted the water down her throat.

The man was still grinning at Casey's amazement. "Say, kid," he said, scratching behind the elephant's ear with a stick, "you wouldn't be lookin' for a job, would ya? How old are ya . . . fourteen? fifteen?"

Casey's mouth dropped open. Had the man said a *job*? "Fourteen," he said eagerly. "Yes, I'd like a job!"

"Good," said the man, leading the elephant back into its place alongside the others and fastening the chain to a stake. "I need a boy 'bout four hours a day to do chores—haul away manure, feed and water, keep 'em clean—stuff like that. It's hard, dirty work. Ever worked with animals before?"

"Yes, sir," Casey said. "My father used to raise horses—we had a farm out near Lancaster. That was before . . ." His voice trailed away.

The man looked at him sharply, but changed the subject. "You goin' ta school?"

Casey wanted to say no, but he slowly nodded yes.

"Well, you come here tomorrow after school and ask for Eph Thompson—that's me. I'll check it out with the circus manager, and if he says okay, I'll pay you fifty cents a day, six days a week . . . *if* you work hard." Eph Thompson extended his hand. "Deal?"

"Deal!" grinned Casey and shook on it. A few minutes later he was standing in front of the two large buildings that served as winter quarters for the Adam Forepaugh Circus, looking for a street name so he could find the place again. There it was: Lehigh Avenue. Then, his heart lighter than it'd been since his father died in a freak riding accident last summer, he took off running toward home. Wait till his mother heard he'd gotten a job! Why, three dollars a week would really help out! Maybe when she realized he could earn money like a man, she'd let him quit school and work full time.

Breathing hard after his two-mile run, Casey fairly ran up the rickety stairs behind the dingy tenement house and burst into the back door of their apartment. "Mama!" he called excitedly. "Mama, guess what! I got a job—"

Casey stopped abruptly. There, standing with Mama in the middle of the sitting room that also served as Mama's sewing room and Casey's bedroom, was his uncle, the Reverend John Watkins, dressed as usual in a drab black coat and clerical collar . . . with another man.

"Casey," Uncle John intoned gravely, "this is the school truant officer."

Chapter 2

Circus Job

CASEY COULDN'T LOOK at his mother's anxious face as he endured the truant officer's lecture about not skipping school anymore. "This is your last warning," the man said finally, putting on his bowler hat. "The next time you will be expelled."

Casey knew the threat was supposed to scare him into staying in school, but getting expelled sounded mighty tempting. . . .

His thoughts were interrupted by the Reverend John Watkins. "I'm ashamed of you, boy!" said his Uncle John sternly as the door closed behind the truant officer. "Why, I used my influence as a min-

ister to get you into a private high school after the death of my brother—God rest his soul—and here you are, ditching school like a common ne'er-do-well. What kind of gratitude is that?"

Casey smoldered. Gratitude? He hadn't wanted his uncle to sell the farm in the first place. He hadn't wanted to move to Philadelphia. He hadn't wanted to go to the stupid academy. Now he was supposed to be thankful? But a pleading look from his mother silenced the biting words on his tongue.

The Reverend Watkins turned on his sister-in-law. "Now, Doreen, you know I didn't approve of Jack marrying a hot-headed Irish Catholic, but what's done is done. And I know my duty to my dead brother's family. At great personal sacrifice, Mary and I have found this apartment for you, put food on your table, and gotten you some sewing work. All I have asked in return is that you attend church regularly, keep your children in line, and don't do anything to bring shame on the good name of Watkins in this city. Now, is that too much to ask?"

Casey could see fire spark in his mother's green eyes. But Doreen Watkins looked at the floor and murmured carefully, "I'll see that Casey stays in school, John."

Satisfied, Reverend Watkins turned to go, then remembered something. "What'd you say about getting a job, Casey?"

Casey hesitated. Uncle John would certainly forbid a Watkins to work for the circus! "Uh . . . j-just helping a man muck out his stables," he stammered.

"After school," he added.

"Hmmm," his uncle frowned. "Might help keep you out of trouble. But," he waggled a forefinger in Casey's face, "schoolwork comes first, you hear?"

✧ ✧ ✧ ✧

"You're not lying to me, are you, Casey?" Mama asked suspiciously when he finally told her a week later that his job of "mucking out stables" was really working as elephant boy at the winter quarters for Forepaugh's Circus.

"Did you really see an elephant?" asked six-year-old Cara, wide-eyed with admiration, as Casey mopped up his supper stew with chunks of crusty bread.

"Not only saw one, I get to take care of *eleven* of 'em!" boasted Casey with his mouth full. "But you keep your mouth shut, Cara—don't you dare tell cousin Elspeth." Elspeth was Aunt Mary and Uncle John's eight-year-old daughter. Little Cara looked up to her cousin like an older sister, but Casey thought Elspeth was stuck-up.

Casey could tell Mama was curious about his new job—once she got over her astonishment. When he described the sleek white horses he'd seen that day doing figure eights in a practice ring, Doreen Watkins got a distant, wistful look in her green eyes.

"See, this guy named Addie Forepaugh trains all sorts of animals . . . tigers, elephants," Casey said, enjoying being the center of attention, "but especially horses. The white horses are his favorites. They do what is called a 'liberty act,' that is, without riders."

"Is Addie the owner of the circus?"

"Nah. That's what I thought, too. But then Eph Thompson—that's the elephant boss—told me some other big outfit bought the circus when Adam Forepaugh, Sr., died a couple years ago. Addie Jr. is the head animal trainer."

"How strange that he didn't inherit his father's circus," Doreen Watkins mused.

"He's got a pretty wife named Lillie . . . calls herself Lillie Deacon," Casey went on. "She does a bareback riding act by herself, and she also works with some other bareback riding ladies—"

"What else do they do in the circus?" Cara interrupted impatiently, tired of all the horse talk.

"Well, I haven't seen too much yet," Casey admitted. "Eph keeps me busy hauling out dirty straw and scrubbing down the elephant pen. But I did see somethin' today that would make your eyes pop out, Cara."

He had been sent to fetch one of the elephant headdresses which was being repaired in the sewing shop in the other building—the one set up with practice rings where the performers practiced their acts. Casey saw a boy about his own age climbing a rope ladder up to a high platform where he unhooked a trapeze bar, then vaulted off the platform, swinging first by his arms, then by his knees . . . back and forth, back and forth, flying silently through the air. Finally the boy let go and somersaulted into a net below.

Casey had stood watching, transfixed. As strange and wonderful as everything connected to the circus had been so far, nothing had made him feel so excited. What did it feel like to fly through the air like that? Casey imagined himself climbing up the rope ladder, catching the trapeze bar, then swinging upside down by his legs. . . .

"Eph Thompson told me the boy is part of an act called The Eugene Brothers," he finished. "Three brothers—they're French or something." His eyes were shining with excitement. "I'd give anything to fly on a trapeze like that," he said dreamily.

Doreen looked at her son sharply. "Now don't go getting any ideas, Casey Watkins," she scolded, collecting the dirty supper dishes and carrying them to the tiny sink. "You heard your Uncle John. School comes first."

School. Casey's mood suddenly darkened. "You don't understand, Mama. It's not the book learnin' that's so hard, but. . . ." How could he tell his mother that getting picked on at school every day was sheer torture? He just didn't fit in.

"I . . . do understand, Casey," Doreen Watkins said gently, pain edging into her voice. It hadn't taken her long to figure out that anti-Irish feelings were high in Philadelphia, the so-called "City of Brotherly Love." It was 1893 and the country was in a recession; jobs were scarce, and "native-born" Americans felt threatened by the flood of new immigrants. Children picked up the prejudices of their parents and unleashed them on the nearest targets—any schoolmate who seemed "different."

Of course, Doreen thought bitterly, Casey and Cara had been born right here in the state of Pennsylvania, and their father, Jack Watkins, was as American as they come. Her mouth tipped in a tiny smile as she remembered the reckless young man she'd married. Jack, son of a Methodist preacher, had been considered "wild," and shocked his family by wanting to raise racehorses. Not only that, he had fallen in love with an Irish lassie named Doreen O'Brien, with rusty-red hair and a natural-born way with horses. Their two children had inherited their mother's eye-catching red hair, ruddy complexion, and faint Irish brogue. But, while Jack Watkins had been alive, no one dared pick on his children or call them names.

Doreen shook off her troubled thoughts and focused her attention back on Casey. "I know it's not easy, son," she sighed, "but your father would want you to go to school. Besides, we need to get along with your Uncle John. He and Mary have done a lot for us."

"*What* have they done for us?" exploded Casey, slamming his fist against the table. "Sold our farm, that's what! Sold all Papa's horses! Why didn't we stay there, Mama? You wanted to—I know you did! But look at you now—stuck in this ugly apartment, crowded into the city, doing sewing for stuck-up ladies—you hate it. I know you do!"

Doreen's eyes filled with tears. "Yes, but . . . your Papa had a lot of debts. He had a plan to pay them off gradual-like, but . . . when he died so sudden . . ." Her voice trembled. "It was the only way, Casey."

Casey turned away. He couldn't stand to see his mother cry. There *had* to be another way.

✧ ✧ ✧ ✧

Casey had been working at the circus winter quarters two weeks when he saw the accident. He was running another errand for Eph Thompson, and, as he usually did, he cut through the big, cavernlike hall to catch a glimpse of the circus performers practicing their acts. Some days it was Addie Forepaugh snapping his whip at the big cats in a huge cage, or the woman named "Zuila" riding her "two-wheeled velocipede" on a high wire, while midgets and clowns seemed to be everywhere practicing their juggling acts and acrobatic jokes.

But today Lillie Deacon, Addie's wife, was in the ring with two other young women working on a difficult horseback ballet. The horses used in the bareback acts were sweet-tempered draft horses, smaller than the workhorses used to haul wagons and heavy equipment, but with nice broad backs and a steady gait.

"No, no, Mimi!" he heard Lillie say to one of the other bareback ladies, who had just tried to vault onto a moving horse but had fallen back into the sawdust. "You're starting too late. Start running when the horse is *here*," she said, pointing to a spot in the ring, "and meet the horse *here*." To illustrate her point, Lillie took a running leap, and with the help of a leather strap on the fancy harness, landed astride the horse's back.

Fascinated, Casey watched. He remembered Mama cutting out her favorite riding horse from the milling herd in their stable yard, grabbing a fistful of mane, and landing on its back—no reins and no saddle. Papa would yell at her that she took too many chances, and besides, women were supposed to ride sidesaddle . . . but Casey could also see the pride in Papa's eyes that his Irish lassie was such a good horsewoman.

As the circus horse loped slowly once more around the ring, Mimi began her run, grabbed the leather strap on the harness, and leaped, this time landing on the horse's back. Lillie and the other circus performers who were watching started to cheer, but Mimi must have tried too hard, because a split second later she fell off the other side.

Immediately there was a thud and a cry of pain. Lillie and several of the clowns rushed over to Mimi's side. Casey heard shouts of "Get the doctor!" and "It might be broken." Casey wanted to stay and see what happened, but he remembered the ointment he was supposed to get from the circus vet for a sore on Queen Victoria's foot. He hustled off.

But on the way back he detoured again through the practice ring to see what had happened. Mimi was gone—they must have taken her to the doctor—

but Lillie Deacon and Addie Forepaugh were arguing in the middle of the ring.

"She broke her ankle?" Addie was yelling angrily. "That's Mimi's third accident in two years!" he fumed, pacing back and forth in his tall boots and riding pants. "She's fired, I tell you. The woman is a hazard."

"It was an *accident*, Addie," Lillie protested. "You can't fire her. We need three bareback riders for our act!"

"*Can't* fire her?" Addie sneered. "A lot of good she'll be to the act in a plaster cast! And I'm not going to pay that woman to just sit around and complain—especially since this is the third time."

"But what am I going to do, Addie?" Lillie cried. "We go on the road in less than two months! How am I going to find another bareback rider now?"

Almost before he realized what he was doing, Casey ran over to the couple in the ring and spoke up, "Mr. Forepaugh, sir? Uh . . . Miss Lillie, ma'am?"

Addie Forepaugh frowned. "Who are you, boy?"

"Casey Watkins, sir. I . . . I work for Eph Thompson, taking care of the elephants. I couldn't help overhearing. If you're looking for a bareback rider, I know someone who is an excellent horsewoman." Casey's heart was beating fast. "She's a real quick learner and . . . well, I know she needs a job."

Chapter 3

Bareback Rider

Y OU'VE TAKEN A JOB doing *what?*" gasped the Reverend John Watkins.

Doreen Watkins, Casey, and Cara were sitting in the Watkins's parlor, dressed in their Sunday best. Casey knew his mother was sick-to-the-stomach nervous, but she'd made him promise that he'd let her do the talking.

"I . . . I've taken a job with Forepaugh's Circus," Doreen said again, twisting the handkerchief in her lap. "Riding horses."

Mary Watkins's face had turned pale. "B-but, Doreen, my dear . . . respectable women simply don't work for a circus—why, it isn't *decent!*"

Casey squirmed. He hoped Aunt

27

Mary wouldn't ask what horseback riders in a circus *wore*. It hadn't seemed so strange to see Lillie Deacon and the other circus women wearing the skimpy outfits needed for acrobatic tricks, but even he had a hard time imagining his mother actually showing her *legs* in public. But still, that was just one little glitch in this whole wild, wonderful idea.

Reverend John Watkins stood up and paced back and forth on the parlor rug. "This is outrageous!" he sputtered, running a hand through his hair. "I overlooked Casey skipping school as the unfortunate but somewhat understandable behavior of a boy who had just lost his father, but . . . but *this*!" He stopped pacing in front of Doreen and glowered at her. "This is a deliberate attempt to embarrass me in this community! My brother's own widow—a showgirl in a circus! Well! If you go ahead with this . . . this wicked idea, I shall never be able to show my face in public again! I will have to resign from my church—"

"Nonsense, John," Mary said, standing up and laying a hand on her husband's arm. "This doesn't have anything to do with *you*. Now let's calm down and talk about the real problems."

Casey arched an eyebrow. *That* showed a little spark. Good for Aunt Mary.

"Now, Doreen," Mary Watkins said, sitting down beside her sister-in-law. "Have you really thought about this? A circus attracts many questionable people. You're a woman alone. What about your safety? And what about the children? Doesn't a circus travel from town to town, just staying a few days in each place? What about their schooling? My dear . . . your husband hasn't even been dead six months yet. I know things have been hard, but . . . things will get better in time." She patted Doreen's hand.

Mary's genuine concern seemed to make Doreen confused. "Well, n-no," Casey's mother stammered slightly, "I . . . haven't thought through everything yet. I signed a contract for only one season—May through October. I thought maybe I could teach the children myself . . . you know, for a few months."

Casey wanted to shout. *Oh, yes!* he thought. If only he didn't have to go to school and face his tormentors even one more day!

His mother twisted her handkerchief. "As for your other concerns, Mary, I . . . well, I don't know how it will work out." Then her eyes flashed and her chin went up. "All I know is that I feel like a prisoner in that tiny little apartment, doing sewing all day! Like I can't breathe!"

At Mary's hurt look, Doreen added hastily, "It's not that I don't appreciate all you and John have done for me, Mary. I do! And if that were the only way, why, I would do what I have to do to manage. But . . ." Doreen glanced at Casey with a little smile. "I've been offered a job. A real job! Working with horses! It's what I do best, Mary and John. Can't you see that?"

"Absolutely not," growled Uncle John. "It's disgraceful! No good will come of this—no good at all. In spite of all our attempts to save your soul, Doreen Watkins, you are choosing to walk the broad path right into hell—and taking your children with you! If you insist on taking this job as a . . . a . . . heathen circus peformer, you will get no more help from us. That's my final word!" Reverend Watkins turned his back and stared out the window through the lacy parlor curtains.

How dare Uncle John talk to his mother like that! Casey opened his mouth to tell his uncle a thing or two, but a firm shake of his mother's head clamped his mouth shut.

Doreen stood up, along with Casey and Cara. "I'm sorry you feel that way, John. I don't want to seem ungrateful, but . . . I *am* going to ride for the circus. I will finish the sewing projects I have already started for your church ladies, and then we will move into circus quarters. You can simply tell people we have moved away."

With that, Doreen marched out of the house and down the sidewalk, the children right on her heels. Casey glanced back anxiously over his shoulder. Were his aunt and uncle going to come after them?

All he saw was cousin Elspeth in the front window, sticking out her tongue.

✧ ✧ ✧ ✧

The end of the railroad car they were given as living quarters was cramped and chilly—it was only March—but Casey didn't really mind. All they did was sleep there and do lessons about two hours a day. Meals were eaten in shifts in the circus mess hall in Building One; the rest of the time, everyone in the circus families worked—even the children. Whenever Doreen wasn't practicing her bareback act with Lillie Deacon, she helped sew costumes or fix plumes on harnesses in the sewing room, or took her turn cleaning up in the mess hall. Cara was too little to be given a regular job, but she stuck close to her mother, picking up sewing scraps or handing supplies to her. And now that Casey was part of the circus family instead of a "townie," he was often called upon to exercise horses, clean harnesses, and run errands between buildings.

"Just you remember, Casey Watkins . . . you're an elephant boy first," grumbled Eph Thompson.

Casey liked Eph. The elephant boss expected Casey to work hard, but Eph was fair and seemed to genuinely like him. Casey quickly learned that Eph also had another passion besides elephants: boxing.

"Ever hear 'bout John Sullivan's famous bareknuckle fight with Jack Kilrain back in '89?" the elephant boss asked one day as he and Casey were outside scrubbing Baby John, one of the smaller elephants, with soapy water and brushes. "Took over two hours, but ol' Sullivan finally got a knockout in the seventy-fifth round!" Eph Thompson chuckled and shook his head. "Man, oh, man, that was some fight."

Casey sloshed a bucket of warm water on Baby John's side. "Is Sullivan still fighting?"

"Oh, yeah . . . but he lost the heavyweight title last year." Eph sounded genuinely sad. "But . . . hey,

I wanna show you something. Back off now."

Casey stood back while Eph grabbed something from inside the big building, then busied himself with the elephant's trunk. Then Eph stood back, clenched his fists, and bounced on the balls of his feet like a boxer. Casey grinned; Baby John was wearing a boxing glove on the end of his trunk. The little elephant shuffled around playfully, then swung the boxing glove and seemed to knock Eph right off his feet. Eph scrambled up and danced around the elphant, punching the air with his fists . . . and fell back again when Baby John again swung his trunk and hit him right in the chest.

Casey shook with laughter. "That's great! You two really look like you're boxing!"

Eph barked a command and the elephant lowered his trunk and stood docilely while Eph scratched his head. "You like it?" the man grinned. "I'm gonna show it to Addie Jr. . . . see if he'll add it to the elephant acts when we go on the road."

"I like it, too," said a boy's voice with a French accent. Casey turned in surprise. The boy who did the trapeze act with The Eugene Brothers was leaning against the open doorway, watching. "It's a great act, Mr. Thompson—Forepaugh would be stupid to turn it down."

Eph's grin widened. "Think so? Well, well . . . say, Ansel, have you met my boy here? Meet Casey Watkins. Casey's ma just got added to the bareback act."

Ansel Eugene held out his hand. "I've seen you watching me when I'm up on the fly bar." The boy was around Casey's age, but had rich dark hair and a tan complexion—a stark contrast to Casey's red hair and ruddy cheeks.

Casey reddened as they shook hands. "Yeah," he admitted. "You're good."

"Would you like me to teach you a few things on

the trapeze?" the other boy asked lightly.

Casey's heart skipped a beat. "You mean it?"

"Sure," Ansel grinned. "We've got a practice bar outside our dressing room. It's only eight feet off the ground, so you can't fall far. Say . . . you busy? I've got some free time now."

To Casey's surprise, Eph shrugged and said, "Yeah, yeah, go on. Just be back in an hour, in time to feed these monsters." With that, Eph and the freshly scrubbed Baby John disappeared back into the animal barn.

✧ ✧ ✧ ✧

Every chance he got, Casey found Ansel and they worked out on the practice bar. Ansel showed him how to get a good swing going, keeping his knees stiff, ankles together, and toes pointed, doing all his bending from the waist. Then Casey practiced throwing his knees over the bar and letting go with his hands, swinging upside down.

"Hey, Ansel, you got yourself a new act?" teased Raoul Eugene, Ansel's next oldest brother, a handsome young man in his twenties.

"Just don't break your neck," growled Pierre, the oldest of the Eugene brothers, watching the boys with one eye as he worked out with hand weights to build muscles in his already bulging arms. The brothers used to travel in Europe with their parents, The Flying Eugenes, but when Forepaugh's Circus asked them to come to America, the senior Eugenes felt they were getting too old for such a trip, so Pierre took over the act.

Casey didn't care about the teasing. He was having too much fun. He imagined himself on the real bars swinging from the roof of the circus tent, the crowds cheering as he did daring feats in the air. He also realized this was the first time since they'd moved to Philadelphia that he'd had a friend. Ansel never made fun of him or called him an "Irish mick." Maybe it was because Forepaugh's circus acts came from all over the world—Mexico, Russia, Spain, Greece . . . even China. *Everyone* was a little bit different.

"See, there're two kinds of trapeze bars," Ansel explained one evening, showing Casey the equipment dangling over the big safety net in the big hall where the circus performers practiced all their acts. "The catch bar is what Pierre uses. He swings by his knees coming from that side, ready to catch Raoul or me when we let go of the fly bar coming from the other side."

Casey went over and tugged on the rope ladder that dangled from the thirty-two foot high platform attached to one of the supporting poles in the big hall. His eyes danced. "Think we could go up there . . . ya know, just to see what it would feel like?" he asked Ansel.

Ansel looked around. The hall was empty. He shrugged. "Well, okay . . . just up to the platform. I could show you how to fall. That's the first thing a trapeze artist has to learn, anyway."

Ansel went up first. As Casey stepped onto the platform and looked down, his stomach suddenly lurched. The ground looked a long way away.

"Don't worry," Ansel grinned, unhooking the fly bar from the pole. "I'll just do a couple swings and then fall into the net. But," he warned, "notice how I kick my legs up as I swing out, so that when I let go I'll fall flat on my back. Otherwise you can hurt yourself."

Casey watched carefully as Ansel fell into the net and bounced a few times. Climbing back down the rope ladder, he joined Ansel as his friend did a somersault off the side of the net.

"Whew!" said Casey, "I didn't realize there was so much to learn about flying on the trapeze. You make it look so easy."

Ansel grinned at the compliment, but his grin faded as they suddenly heard voices arguing just outside the hall. The boys quietly went closer and peeked through the archway. They could see Pierre Eugene and the fat circus manager, Joe McCaddon, standing in the passageway.

"A raise?" McCaddon was yelling, a cigar hanging out one side of his mouth. "Are you out of your crazy mind? This circus lost money last year! We have another season to prove ourselves or the owners threaten to sell us out. Now, does that sound like I can give you flyin' Frenchies more money?"

"Now wait a minute, McCaddon," protested Ansel's brother. "We've been with this circus four years. Our contract with Forepaugh Sr. calls for a raise each year we stay with the circus."

"Yeah, but that was before the old man died," snarled McCaddon. "We're under new management now, remember? Besides, why should we give you a raise? The World's Fair booking in Chicago is comin' up in June—people will be comin' from all over the world. It's a chance to impress people big time, maybe pull this circus out of the skids. But you Eugenes are doin' the same act you did last year. Nothin' new— nothing to get the crowds excited. In fact, instead of a raise, maybe we oughta cut you out now!" With that, the circus manager stomped off, puffing on his cigar.

Casey heard Pierre Eugene swear under his breath. What was going on? The boy turned, wide-eyed, toward his friend . . . but Ansel had disappeared.

Chapter 4

Circus Flyer

THE NEXT DAY, a worried Casey told Eph Thompson what he'd overheard and asked if he thought McCaddon would really cut out the Eugene Brothers act.

Eph shrugged. "I dunno. Everybody's jumpy right about now, trying to finalize the best acts before we  go on the road. But . . . nah, don't think so. It's too late to get any new acts at this late date. Your mama was a lucky find for the bareback act. Man, oh, man, she does add sizzle to that act," the elephant handler chuckled.

Casey grinned. His mama was good, no doubt about that. He was proud of the way she'd quickly caught on to the bareback stunts . . . even spiced them up with a few ideas of her own.

Then he remembered something. "Say, Eph, did you show your John Sullivan boxing act to Mr. Forepaugh? What'd he say?"

Eph went over and leaned against Baby John as the elephant stood in place, half asleep. "Well, now, I thought you'd never ask. Casey Watkins, you are looking at the newest, hottest elephant act on this side of the Mississippi—maybe the other side, too."

"Wahoo!" Casey yelped, punching the air. "That's great, Eph! So Addie Jr. liked it, huh?"

Eph got a funny look on his face. "Well . . . that's a little hard to tell," he admitted. "I showed him the act, but he didn't say anything about it . . . just started yelling at me for training one of the elephants without his say-so. But while we were yelling at each other, Joe McCaddon came along, chomping on that cigar of his, and wanted to know what was goin' on. When I told him, he asked to see the act. I couldn't believe it; that mean ol' face actually cracked a smile when Baby John here knocked me down for the count. Even took the cigar out of his mouth, pointed it at Addie Forepaugh, and *ordered* him to add the boxing act to the road show. Said something about needing just this sort of thing to wow the crowds in Chicago." Eph shook his head. "Addie Jr. ain't too happy, though, getting overruled like that. Head animal trainer has *always* had final say over which animal acts go on the road."

Casey nodded. This circus business was more

complicated than he had realized. His worry deepened when he didn't see Ansel all that day, but the next day Ansel showed up unexpectedly while Casey was watching his mother putting some of the bareback horses through their paces. Ansel grabbed Casey's arm and eagerly pulled him toward the Eugenes' dressing room.

"Hurry up, Casey," he said. "My brother wants to see you."

Uh-oh, thought Casey. *Pierre saw me up on that platform, and I'm gonna get it.* On the other hand, he told himself, if Pierre was mad, why was Ansel so excited?

When they got to the dressing room, Pierre Eugene didn't say anything at first . . . just looked Casey up and down. Nervous, Casey looked at Raoul Eugene, but Ansel's middle brother glanced away and busied himself wrapping wristbands on his arms.

Finally Pierre uncrossed his arms and put his hands on his slender hips. "So . . . your name is Watkins? Casey Watkins? What kind of Irish name is *Watkins*?"

Casey opened his mouth to explain, but Pierre went right on.

"So, Casey Watkins, you think you want to be a flyer?"

"Uh, n-no . . . I mean, well, yes, sir," he stammered. "Someday I'd sure like to be a trapeze flyer as good as you and Ansel and Raoul." Then Casey reddened. He hadn't meant to sound so arrogant.

"So? What about now?" asked Pierre. "No better

time to learn than when you're young."

Startled, Casey looked at Ansel. Was Pierre making fun of him? But Ansel just grinned as his older brother continued.

"I'm askin' if you'd like to be part of the Eugene Brothers, Watkins—develop a new act for the upcomin' season. I've seen you work out with Ansel on the practice bar. Not bad for a beginner. See, I've got this idea for a stunt called the double pass . . . but it needs someone about the same size and weight as Ansel here, and you sure do fit the bill. . . ."

Casey felt light-headed as Pierre Eugene's voice droned on. *Become a circus flyer?* He never imagined his dream would really come true. But . . . the circus was going on the road in another month! How could he ever learn how to do it right in such a short time?

✧ ✧ ✧ ✧

Doreen Watkins didn't approve of this nonsense. "Leave the flying to the Eugenes," she snapped at Casey after Pierre had approached her about his idea. "I don't want you to get hurt." The Watkins were sitting at the small table in their cramped quarters in the railroad car, trying to finish up the morning's school lessons.

"But, Mama," argued Casey, "I won't get hurt. The Eugenes always use a safety net. Ansel even said the first thing a trapeze artist learns is how to fall right."

"Mama, is Casey going to fall?" asked Cara anx-

41

iously, tugging on her mother's riding tunic. Doreen had sewn a loose, knee-length, blue tunic to go over her shirt and riding tights for practice sessions. Several of the clowns had made rude remarks about her attempt at modesty, but Doreen just tossed her mane of thick hair and ignored them.

"Not fall *by accident*, silly," Casey said, yanking one of Cara's braids. "Fall *on purpose*—there's a big difference."

"But what about your school lessons?" his mother went on. "Learning to do a trapeze act on short notice is going to be a full-time job . . . not to mention keeping up with your job taking care of the elephants—which brings in extra money, remember."

Casey evaded his mother's question. He was already having a hard time concentrating on books when so much excitement was going on in the winter quarters.

"I know it's crazy, Mama, but just give me a chance," he pleaded. "It's something I gotta try. I might never get another opportunity like this."

In the end, Casey finally won his mother's reluctant permission to let Pierre Eugene teach him. It was harder convincing the circus manager. *What?* Joe McCaddon blustered. "Take this greenhorn kid here and put him up on the trapeze? You're crazy, Eugene. Sure, I know we hired his mother on short notice, but at least she's an experienced rider. This kid doesn't know nothin'!"

But Pierre Eugene convinced him it wouldn't hurt to try. If it worked, he argued, they'd have an exciting new act for the Chicago World's Fair. *That* got McCaddon's attention. "Well, okay," he muttered. "But I'm not paying the kid a cent extra until I see him actually perform up there."

With only four weeks until the circus packed up and began the performance season, Pierre worked Casey hard every day. The first time Casey's feet left the platform and he swung out into space on the trapeze bar, fear seemed to rush into every pore. Even wearing the "mechanic"—a safety line attached to a belt around his waist—he was so scared he thought he was going to lose his lunch. But Ansel was right: Pierre made Casey fall into the net again and again and again before he worked on any other technique.

In order to do his chores for Eph Thompson and be ready when the Eugenes got a time slot to practice in the big hall, Casey had to get up while it was still dark to muck out the elephant quarters, haul away the old straw and manure, and lay down fresh straw. Later he had to come back to make sure the eleven elephants had enough feed and fresh water. Even then, Eph complained that the Eugenes were "stealing" his elephant boy.

"You think Queen Victoria here wants her dinner at three in the afternoon?" he grumbled. "Don't forget who hired you first, boy."

"Aw, come on, Eph," said Casey. "Give me a break. You and Baby John are getting a chance to do your boxing act. I just want a chance to do this flying act, too. We gotta support each other, now, don't we?"

"Humph, that's different," said Eph . . . but he did wander by to watch Casey learning how to swing by his knees on the fly bar.

Casey's stomach still seemed to tie up in a big knot every time Pierre Eugene showed him the next trick he was supposed to learn. One late evening, when his trainer said it was time to learn to "fly"— that is, let go and be caught by the catcher—to Casey's relief they started on the practice bar outside the dressing room.

"This routine is called 'hocks off,' " Pierre said, hoisting Casey up with his strong hands till the boy had a grip on the bar. "Get a good swing going . . . that's right. Keep those knees together and don't bend 'em. All right, throw your legs up, get more height. Now, swing your legs over the bar and let go with your hands like we've been practicing . . . that's right. Don't slow down! Keep a good swing going! Okay, Watkins, on your next forward swing, I want you to stretch out your arms, grab my wrists, and let go with your legs . . . *now!*"

Casey hesitated a fraction of a second too long . . . and would have landed on the hard-packed dirt floor if Pierre hadn't caught him.

"Never mind," the Frenchman said brusquely. "Get back on that bar and do it again."

When Casey managed to get his "hocks" off the bar and grab Pierre's wrists ten times in a row, the weary crew quit for the night.

"Boy's comin' along, Eugene," drawled a voice from the shadows. It was Joe McCaddon. How long

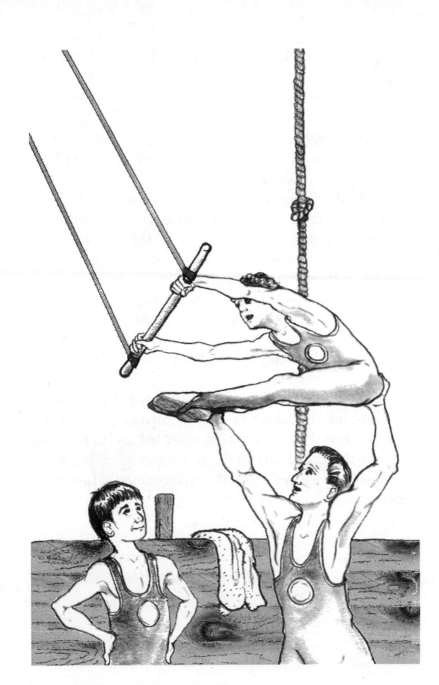

had *he* been watching? "But I'd say he has a long way to go before you've got yourselves an act," the circus manager scoffed. "Only two weeks till this outfit hits the road, ya know."

Pierre Eugene didn't answer. He just threw Casey a towel to dry off with, then slammed the door of the dressing room behind him.

At that moment, Casey was so tired and sore he didn't even care what McCaddon thought. He just wanted to crawl into his bunk in the railroad car. The April night was chilly and damp, a low cover of clouds hid any light from the moon or stars. As Casey wearily picked his way through the shadows of the railroad siding, he thought he heard noises near their sleeping car . . . then a man's throaty laughter, and his mother's angry voice: "Let go of my arm!"

"Hey!" yelled Casey, running toward the voices. Just outside the door of their railroad car, a burly figure seemed to be scuffling with his mother. Casey lit into the man, hitting him angrily with his fists. "Leave my mother alone!" he screamed. "Let go of her!"

Chapter 5

On the Road

HUH? WHAT'S THIS!" the man laughed, letting go of Doreen Walker's arm and giving Casey a shove that sent him sprawling to the ground. "The tiger cub's got his hackles up, eh? Calm down, kid. I wasn't hurtin' your mother none . . . jest wanted a lil' ol' kiss."

Doreen quickly swung up onto the steps of the sleeping car. "Problem is, buster," she bristled, "your attentions aren't welcome. I told you before—leave me alone! Come on, Casey."

Casey hurriedly scrambled into the car after her. Cara had been watching wide-eyed from the window, and started to cry when Doreen and Casey plopped down on their bunks.

"Who is he, Mama?" Casey demanded, still angry that someone had dared bother his mother.

Doreen gave a nervous laugh as she cuddled Cara. "Oh, just one of the roustabouts McCaddon hired recently . . . name's Tucker. He's been flirting with me for days. I tried to ignore him, but tonight he got persistent. I'm glad you came along when you did, Casey. But . . . don't worry. I don't think he'll bother me again."

Casey had been so busy concentrating on the trapeze lessons that he hadn't really paid attention to the increased activity around the winter quarters as the circus got ready to go on the road. Working-men—nicknamed "roustabouts"—were being hired to do the setting up and taking down of the circus at each stop. Clowns were walking around in whiteface and odd clothes as each one put the final touches on his or her "clown character" for the coming season. Costumes were being decorated with sequins and plumes and fitted for the last time.

Casy felt badly that he'd been ignoring his mother and little sister, but there wasn't much he could do about it. Practice sessions with the Eugene brothers increased. He moved from the practice bar outside the dressing room to the fly bar over the big net to do the "hocks off" routine. Sometimes his timing was just right, and he felt a thrill of accomplishment as he swung through the air in Pierre's strong grasp. But too often his timing was off or he didn't get enough height to his swing, and he landed in the net.

Still, one day Pierre said it was time to learn the

double pass. "Ansel will do the hard work," he told Casey. "He'll come to me first from the fly bar . . . then when Raoul gives you the signal, you swing toward me on the fly bar, just like you do for 'hocks off.' Except, when you let go with your legs and reach for my wrists, I'm gonna be throwing Ansel back to the fly bar you just left—you'll be passing in midair."

Casey was shaking terribly the first time they tried it. He knew his part was just like "hocks off," but . . . what if his timing was off? Ansel had to do a full twist somersault coming back . . . what if he and Ansel collided in midair? Casey was so afraid of hitting Ansel that he pulled back his arms, missed Pierre's outstretched hands, and landed in the net.

"Don't worry about Ansel!" Pierre shouted down at him from the catch bar. "Just do what *you're* supposed to do!"

Casey rolled off the net and went back up to the platform. Again and again he tried, but something always seemed to go wrong.

The last week was dress rehearsal. The circus performers did all their acts in the order they would appear on the program, including the Spectacle just before intermission—a reenactment entitled "The American Revolution, Scenes and Battles of 1776," complete with Redcoats and booming cannons. Almost all the circus performers took part in the massive spectacle, including all three Watkins dressed up like an early American family helping to pull down the statue of King George III. But since Casey wasn't ready on the trapeze yet, The Eugene Brothers rehearsed their act without the double pass.

At dawn on April 30 Casey woke up to shouts and curses; the roustabouts were already loading equipment onto the flatcars. All day Addie Forepaugh galloped back and forth along the railroad siding on horseback, personally supervising the loading of the caged animals and his beloved horses. Eph Thompson demanded that Casey be available all day for getting the elephants settled in their travel quarters.

Casey might have enjoyed the excitment of the circus getting ready to pull out of Philadelphia at midnight . . . except for one thing.

He knew he wasn't ready to do the double pass at the circus's first scheduled road performance May 3.

❖ ❖ ❖ ❖

"What do you mean, the act isn't ready!" Joe McCaddon growled, the end of his cigar glowing red with each word. "We made a deal, remember?"

"I think you remember it wrong," Pierre Eugene said calmly. The two big buildings that housed Forepaugh's winter quarters were all but empty and dark, except for the sputtering oil lamp in the manger's office. "I said we'd have a spectacular new act for the World's Fair . . . and we're not due in Chicago till June. That's five weeks, and I promise you, McCaddon, the act will be ready."

Casey shifted nervously as the circus manager's eyes darted from one to the other of the three Eugene brothers and their protégé. The ever-present cigar bobbed up and down as McCaddon digested this information.

"Humph!" he finally sputtered. "When do you think you're gonna practice? We got performances, remember? Two a day! An' when we're not perform-ing, we're travelin'."

A faint smile tugged at the trapeze artist's mouth. "That's my problem," he said. "Oh, by the way . . . my idea is to bill Ansel and Casey here as 'The Eugene Twins—doing the sensational double pass.' Whadd'ya think?"

"Ha!" jeered McCaddon. "Twins? These two look about as alike as a pig and a poodle. Ain't nobody gonna think this red-haired Irish kid is French."

"Oh, I don't know," grinned Pierre. "A little black hair dye can go a long way foolin' a crowd . . . especially from a distance."

A few hours later, Casey stood in the dark at the half-closed door of the sleeping car which had earlier been hooked to the other circus cars with mighty bumps and grinds. Only Cara was asleep in their car; everyone else was too wound up.

Casey was both disappointed and relieved that "the Eugene Twins" act had been put on hold. He felt like he'd let the Eugene brothers down. But, five weeks—surely he'd be able to do it in five weeks! After all, Ansel had said that the World's Fair in Chicago was the 1893 season's biggest booking; that was what *really* counted.

Oh, if only Papa could see me now, Casey thought.

Working for a circus . . . taking care of elephants . . . practicing on a flying trapeze. . . . Suddenly a great wave of loneliness for his father washed over him. Even if he got the act down pat, Papa would never see him, would never know.

Just then Casey's mother came up and leaned on the half-open door beside him. She didn't say anything, just laid a reassuring hand on his shoulder. They felt the train shudder and squeal as it slowly pulled out of the railroad siding.

Excitement soon replaced the boy's brooding thoughts. The Great Forepaugh Circus Train was leaving town while the rest of the city slept. And Casey Watkins was on board!

❖ ❖ ❖ ❖

One problem with being part of a circus, Casey realized as the enormous canvas circus tent went up in the first town, was that he'd never actually get to see the circus from start to finish. In fact, except for the Grand Parade at the beginning and his small part in the 1776 Spectacle, he was supposed to wait with Eph and the elephants in the "backyard"—the area just outside the performers' entrance into the big circus tent—to be sure the big beasts were ready to go into the ring when it was time for the elephant acts. But at least Eph relented and let him duck back into the big top to see his mother perform.

Casey sucked in his breath when the bareback riders came into the far ring of the two-ring circus.

Doreen, Lillie, and Magda, the third female bareback rider, wore short, sparkling blue outfits with blue velvet boots, their hair tucked under soft, blue velvet caps. The dapple-gray horses, decorated with blue plumes and velvet-trimmed harnesses, loped calmly around the ring as the three women leaped on and off their backs, stood on their heads, and did somersaults off the tail end. Casey grinned as the crowd clapped and whistled its approval.

He desperately wanted to see Eph and Baby John do their John L. Sullivan boxing match act for the first time, but he had to stay with the other elephants. By the roars of laughter and stamping of feet inside the tent, however, he could tell it was a big success.

Immediately after the second show was over and the evening crowd had emptied from the tent, Casey found out when The Eugene Brothers were going to practice the new double pass: late at night, when the rest of the circus performers were tumbling into bed. When his mother tried to wake him for "school lessons" the next morning, he was so tired he rolled over and refused to get up.

Pretty soon, life on the road fell into a sort of routine, but each day still held an edge of excitement for Casey. The circus train slowly snaked its way west through Pennsylvania, Ohio, and Indiana, staying in one place anywhere from two days to one week, depending on the size of the town. When the last performance was over, the circus broke down, loaded up, and pulled out of town in the middle of the night, heading for the next booking.

After a few futile attempts to keep up with Casey's school lessons, Doreen Watkins gave up. Casey tried to ignore her disappointment; he knew it was hard keeping up with family life with two performances a day and so little privacy in their cramped quarters. But, he told himself, wasn't this better than that miserable apartment in Philadelphia, with Uncle John breathing hell and damnation down their necks?

The one thing he continued to worry about, however, was the man named Tucker. Many of the showgirls flirted right back with the circus workers who hung around, whistling and making comments. Doreen Watkins, however, kept to herself and made few friends, except for an admiring respect for Lillie Deacon . . . but her very reserve seemed to egg on men like Tucker, who enjoyed teasing and needling her, just to get her dander up.

Even though the huge tent could seat ten thousand, the crowds were sometimes only half that. Still, the spectators loved Addie Forepaugh's famous horse, Blondin, who walked a plank disguised to look like a tightrope. Johnny Purvis, Forepaugh's "boss clown," and his troupe of joeys kept the crowd laughing in between acts. There was even a "Wild West" act featuring Dr. Bill Carver, a champion rifle shot and ex-partner of the famous Buffalo Bill Cody.

The small crowds were a disappointment, however, to Ben Lusbie, Forepaugh's illustrious ticket seller, a suave-looking man with a trim, black mus-

tache who could sell five thousand tickets in an hour. In order to generate excitement, he often delayed the sale of tickets until the last hour before the show. When he finally opened the window of the gaily painted "4-Paws Ticket Wagon" parked outside the main entrance of the circus, people were clamoring to get their tickets and Lusbie sold them lightning fast.

"Notice anything?" Ansel said under his breath to Casey as the two boys watched Lusbie selling tickets one morning in a mid-sized town in Ohio. At first Casey didn't know what his friend meant . . . then he noticed some of Lusbie's men going through the crowd yelling, "Hurry! Hurry! Get your tickets now before they're sold out!" Other assistants then went through the crowd, offering the fifty-cent tickets to anxious circus-goers for an additional ten cents. "If you wait in line for the regular price, you might miss out," they were told seriously.

"Is that *legal?*" Casey asked skeptically.

Ansel shrugged. "I dunno . . . but I'm sure *that* isn't." He jerked his head toward the dashing Ben Lusbie, who kept up a fast running chatter like an auctioneer: "Fiveticketssirhere'syourchangemoveon-nowmakewayforthefolksbehindyou . . . ." Usually the excited men, women, and children grabbed their tickets and stuffed the change back in their pockets without counting it. And the local pickpockets, who seemed to materialize out of thin air whenever the circus came to town, watched which pocket the money went into and happily lifted it out.

Casey was astonished. "Why doesn't Joe McCaddon do something about this? The people are getting cheated, or pickpocketed . . . or both."

Ansel shrugged again. "If he knows about it, he looks the other way. Most circus people figure it's all a game. We give 'em a good show, and they leave their money behind."

Casey didn't tell his mother what he'd learned about ticket selling. Doreen Watkins was honest down to the soles of her feet, and sometimes she even embarrassed Casey by marching back to a store if a clerk gave her a penny too much in change. He didn't want to give her any more reason to be unhappy about circus life . . . not before he had a chance to perfect the double pass and make his debut at the Chicago World's Fair.

And the late-night practices *were* paying off. At their last stop in Indiana before the circus train headed around the bottom of Lake Michigan toward Chicago, Pierre casually told Casey the act was ready and sent him to his mother to get his hair dyed.

"Eph! Eph!" he cried excitedly, running into the tent where the elephants were stabled, black dye still staining his neck. "Guess what! I finally get to do the Eugene Twins act at the . . ."

His voice died away as he saw Eph Thompson and Addie Forepaugh arguing angrily. The head animal trainer glanced in Casey's direction, then turned back to the elephant boss. "I don't care if you don't like it, Thompson, that's just the way it's gonna be." Then Forepaugh turned on the heels of his riding boots and stalked out of the tent.

Casey slowly walked closer. "Eph? What did Mr.

Forepaugh want?" He could see both hurt and anger in the man's eyes. "What's wrong, Eph?"

Eph kicked a nearby bucket, and the sleepy elephants shuffled nervously. "That dirty rat just took over my act, that's what," he spit out.

"What? The John L. Sullivan act? But why? That's *your* act, Eph!"

"Humph. We're hitting the World's Fair tomorrow, that's why. Circus crowd's gonna be full of foreigners, all of 'em either rich or famous. Forepaugh wants the act for himself!"

Chapter 6

Chicago World's Fair

FINDING OUT THAT EPH'S popular boxing act had been taken over by Addie Forepaugh took the wind out of Casey's good news. It wasn't fair! He wanted Eph to be happy, too. Still, his excitement mounted as the circus train pulled into Chicago. The "World's Columbian Exposition," as the World's Fair was officially called, had just opened in May, and the city seemed electric.

Crowds gathered to watch as teams of elephants and draft horses strained in their harnesses to pull up the big circus tents along Chicago's lakefront. Besides the main tent used for performances, several other tents housed Forepaugh's menagerie of exotic animals, plus horses, elephants, other performing animals, dressing rooms, and a mess tent.

Casey and Cara were awed by the sight of Lake Michigan. "It looks like an ocean!" Cara said, her eyes dancing. The children, dressed in their costumes, were waiting in the hot sun as circus performers, animals, and fancy wagons lined up for the Grand Parade through the city streets. The lake behind them was so big, it was impossible to see the shoreline on the other side. Ansel wasn't so impressed; he had seen the real ocean when he had come to the United States on a ship.

"But where's the fair?" Casey wondered out loud. Except for the lake, all he could see from the corner of Madison Street and Michigan Avenue where the circus was set up were sober-looking office buildings several stories high, men in top hats and waistcoats bustling along the sidewalks, electric streetcars, and horses pulling fancy carriages through the streets.

"South of the city, I think . . . some place called Jackson Park," Ansel said. He and Casey were dressed in matching costumes of bright yellow tops and leggings, red sashes, and red-and-yellow capes with sparkling red sequins in great swirls. Pierre and Raoul were the same, except they had blue sashes and blue-and-yellow capes. "I heard McCaddon grumbling about Buffalo Bill's Wild West Show getting the choice spot right across from the entrance to the fair," Ansel added.

Casey was disappointed. He was hoping he'd get to see the World's Fair while they were in Chicago. He had heard the other circus performers talk about wonders from all over the world—new-fangled machines, thousands of electric lights, motorcars, model villages from places like Egypt and Japan and Samoa, even a Viking ship! But most of all, he'd heard rumors about a magnificent wheel, three times as tall as the circus tent, that a person could ride on and see the whole city.

But he didn't have much time to think about the fair right then, because the parade master was blowing his whistle and the band, riding on one of the fancy wagons, was striking up a tune. Casey saw Eph Thompson standing at the head of his line of elephants and felt a little guilty. He'd always walked with Eph and the elephants in the parade . . . but today he was walking with The Eugene Brothers.

Casey tried to shrug it off. He felt badly for Eph, but it wasn't his fault Eph's act had been stolen by Addie Forepaugh. Right now he had to think about his own debut tomorrow as one of the "Eugene Twins," doing the spectacular double pass.

Cheering crowds lined the sidewalks as the colorful parade wound through downtown Chicago. The great tableau floats, like "Saint George and the Dragon" and "Cleopatra's Barge," were pulled by prancing horses, followed by dogs walking on their hind legs, comical clowns, beautiful horses and costumed riders, cages of lions and tigers and other strange animals like the amazing hippo. Bringing up

61

the rear of the parade was the steam calliope, piping out its cheerful tunes.

Casey felt proud as boys his own age gaped in admiration as The Eugene Brothers walked by in their swirling capes, smiling and waving at the crowd. But as the parade wound through streets named Adams . . . Fulton . . . Paulina . . . LaSalle . . . the capes began to feel heavy and hot in the midmorning sun. He wiped sweat from his forehead, hoping the dark dye in his hair wasn't streaking down his face.

As the parade turned from Rush Street onto Michigan Avenue for the last leg, a strange boxy wagon on a side street caught Casey's eye. It looked almost like a horse-drawn hearse, except the window curtains were pulled back, and a stout, middle-aged man with white chin whiskers was standing on the driver's seat with a boy about Casey's age, wide smiles on their faces. Casey saw the man and the boy climb down and push their way to the front of the crowd lining the sidewalk.

To Casey's surprise, the man with the white whiskers hailed him as The Eugene Brothers walked by. "Hello! You there, boy!" he called in a friendly voice, catching Casey's eye. "Do you have any shows on Sunday?"

Casey was surprised the man should single him out. He squared his shoulders and called back proudly, "Yes! Two every day!"

"Morning or afternoon?" the man called back, running a little alongside as the parade moved on.

"Afternoon and evening!" Casey grinned. It was funny to see the stout man walking so fast.

"Excellent!" the man beamed. "Who's your manager?"

Casey just had time to yell back, "Joe McCaddon!" before the parade swept him out of the man's sight. He looked at Ansel and shrugged. That was strange . . . what did the man want? He had a boy with him. Maybe they just wanted to come see the circus. But he didn't need to see the manager if he just wanted a couple of tickets.

When the parade finally arrived at the circus lot, Casey hurriedly shed his costume and put on his work pants and shirt. "Casey," his mother called into the dressing room, "I want you to look after Cara—"

"Can't, Mama," he said. "I gotta help Eph feed and water the elephants." Before his mother could protest, Casey headed for the elephant tent. Actually, Eph hadn't asked him to, but he didn't want Eph to think he'd abandoned his job just because he was now doing a trapeze act. Eph only grunted when Casey grabbed a couple buckets and headed for the water barrels, but he knew the elephant boss was pleased that he'd shown up.

As Casey hauled his fifth load of water toward the elephant tent, he suddenly saw that strange wagon again, its horse tied near the main tent. This time he could read the words along its side: "D. L. Moody . . . The Bible Institute, Chicago." *What?* he thought. *Was the guy some kind of preacher or something?*

He looked around. Sure enough, there were the stout man and lanky boy talking to the circus manager. Curious, Casey edged closer to the little group.

"You gotta be kidding, Moody," McCaddon was saying, blowing clouds of cigar smoke in the man's face. "Let you use my circus tent for a preaching service? Ha, ha . . . this is your idea of a joke, right?"

"No, no joke at all," said the man courteously. "We have a big evangelistic campaign going on in Chicago this summer, running neck and neck with the World's Fair, and we're in need of a facility such as your tent for the large crowds we are drawing."

"Large crowds?" guffawed McCaddon. "You're over your head, Moody. This tent seats ten thousand! We plan to fill it up twice a day while we're here in Chicago. But I ain't *never* seen no preacher draw a crowd like The Greatest Show on Earth . . . ha, ha!"

Mr. Moody shrugged and smiled. "I am prepared to pay you a reasonable rate for the use of your tent. Are we talking business?"

"Pay?" said Joe McCaddon, his tone changing. "That's different. Why didn't ya say so? When did ya say ya wanna use it? Sundays? Hmmm . . ." The cigar bobbed up and down. "We'll be here June eleventh . . . an' the eighteenth. Two Sundays. An' we got shows at two and eight P.M."

"That would work perfectly," said Mr. Moody, a smile wiggling his whiskers. "Shall we say . . . ten A.M. on the eleventh and the eighteenth?"

As the two men discussed details, the boy with Mr. Moody noticed Casey and wandered over. "Hi," he said. "My name is Paul Moody. You're with the circus, right?"

Casey nodded. He wondered if the boy recognized him from the parade . . . and was suddenly embarrassed by his dirty work clothes. "These are just, uh . . . I'm actually with The Eugene Brothers trapeze act." The words felt funny rolling off his tongue, but the other boy seemed impressed.

"Now I remember—you were in the parade! I've never seen a circus," he said wistfully. "Wish I could see you do your act."

Casey felt better. The boy *did* recognize him. Just then Mr. Moody shook hands with Joe McCaddon and swung jauntily toward the boys. "All set, Paul," he said, looking pleased with himself. "Say," he added, noticing Casey. "You're the young man we talked to in the parade, right?"

"Yes, sir."

"Well," beamed Mr. Moody, hands clasped behind his back. "Are you going to come to my show Sunday morning? Right here in Forepaugh's circus tent!"

Casey grinned. The man seemed friendly enough, even if he was a preacher. "Sure," he said saucily, "if you'll come to *my* show on Saturday. Two o'clock or eight—take your pick!"

The stout man tipped back his head and laughed heartily. "A real businessman, eh? You drive a hard bargain. Ha, ha . . . not unlike myself at your age." He leaned toward Casey, a twinkle in his eye. "It's a deal, young man. I'll come to your show . . . you come to my show. Shake on it?" And he held out his hand.

Casey's grin widened as he shook the man's hand.

"Really, Papa? We're going to the circus?" he

heard Paul Moody say happily as the pair walked back toward the funny wagon. "Are you sure Mr. Sankey and the others . . ."

As he watched the father and son go off together, Casey had a strange, lonely feeling inside. He grabbed the two buckets at his feet and hurried back to the elephant tent.

Chapter 7

Ferris's Big Wheel

COME ON, CASEY!" Ansel called from outside the Watkins's makeshift dressing room, which the family was also using for sleeping in the muggy Chicago weather. "McCaddon wants all the men and boys out on the streets, passing out circus flyers. Hurry up!"

It was Saturday morning, and Casey had been so excited last night thinking about his debut with The Eugene Brothers that it had taken him hours to fall asleep. Now he sat up, still half asleep, and groggily started pulling on his boots.

"Oh, Mama, can I go, too?" Cara begged, grabbing her mother's brush and trying to take the snarls out of her thick, curly hair.

"Just men and boys, stupid," growled Casey . . . then he saw the hurt look on his sister's face. "Sorry," he muttered. He didn't know why he was in such a surly mood. Not enough sleep, he guessed.

"You stay with Ansel or the other men, you hear?" his mother called after him as Casey stumbled out of the tent into the bright sunlight.

Joe McCaddon was standing in front of the main tent, handing a stack of flyers to every man and boy he could round up. "I want these flyers all over this city," he said. "There's a big movement in this city to prohibit shows like ours from playing on Sunday— they're even giving the World's Fair a hard time." A mocking smile cracked his face. "But this flyer oughta get 'em out. Now . . . you men take the north section . . . you fellas over here, take the west section of the city . . . and you men, head south."

Ansel and Casey looked at each other and grinned. They were assigned to the south section. This was their chance to see the World's Fair! But . . . they each needed a nickle for the streetcar and fifty cents to get into the fair. Casey thought about asking his mother for the money, but knew she'd never give it to him. After a whispered consultation, the two boys approached the circus manager.

"Mr. McCaddon? We think passing out flyers in-side the fair—you know, where all the people are— would attract a lot more of them to the circus," Casey said with more confidence than he actually felt.

"Ya do, eh?" said Joe McCaddon suspiciously. "How d'ya figure?"

"Well, sir," said Casey, "if we only pass these out on the streets of Chicago, we may just run into the average workingman or housewife. The people inside the fair, on the other hand, are probably people with money and time for amusement. So going into the fair itself would be a good, um, investment."

"Huh? Investment? What're ya talking about?"

"Er . . . fifty-five cents, sir," said Ansel. "Each."

"Well, I'll be jibbered," Joe McCaddon muttered under his breath. He eyed the boys. "But . . . ya do have a point."

To the boys' surprise, they soon found themselves riding a streetcar for Jackson Park, with fifty cents each in their pockets and a large stack of flyers to pass out.

"Hey, look at this," Casey said loudly over the rattle of the streetcar, holding up a copy of the flyer for Ansel to see.

Ha! Ha! Ha!
Three Big SHOWS!
Moody in the morning.
Forepaugh in the afternoon
and evening.

"Oh, boy," whistled Ansel. "That Mr. Moody is gonna be mad when he sees this. McCaddon has some nerve making fun of a preacher."

"Yeah," Casey agreed. "It's not like him to give anybody free advertising, either. He must figure it'll catch people's attention and be good for business."

Casey and Ansel had to scrunch over on the wooden seats as more and more fairgoers climbed on—men in bowler hats, starched collars, and neckties; women in straw hats and pretty dresses. Even the children were dressed up. A girl that reminded Casey of cousin Elspeth stared at the boys for a minute, then stuck out her tongue.

Casey was tempted to yell at her that they were the famous Eugene Twins from the circus and they wouldn't let her in, even if she bought a ticket . . . but thought better of it. No one would believe him.

When the streetcar finally jerked to a stop at Fifty-fifth Street on the south side, Ansel and Casey squeezed off and started handing out flyers to the other passengers as they got off. It made him mad when several people glanced at the flyer, then tossed it on the ground. He quickly picked up the discarded papers and ran after Ansel who was heading for the main gate.

Even from the gate, Casey was dazzled by the elegant, white buildings he could see inside the fairgrounds. On his left the lake sparkled jade green in the sun. Spires and statues and enormous buildings stretched in front of him as far as the eye could see. And off to his right . . .

That's when Casey saw the Wheel. Even from several blocks away, it seemed to hover like a bicycle wheel for the clouds, taller than anything he'd ever imagined. He pulled Ansel away from the ticket booth. "Look," he pointed. "I gotta ride it! I just gotta."

"But we only have fifty cents to get into the fair," Ansel pointed out.

"I know . . . that's why we have to find another way in."

The ticket sellers were watching the main gate like hawks, so Casey and Ansel headed down Stoney Island Avenue along the west side of the fair. A couple blocks south, some workmen had opened part of the fencing to remove some dead shrubbery from the landscaping. Seeing their opportunity, Casey and Ansel ducked into the opening and ran into the fairgrounds, ignoring the workmen's shouts.

Casey knew his mother would throw a fit if she knew he was at the fair, much less had snuck in. But he shrugged off his guilty feelings. He was here on business for Forepaugh's Circus, wasn't he?

The two boys walked around the north end of the fair, cheerfully passing out the circus flyers advertising the Sunday shows and gawking at the enormous Palace of Fine Arts and buildings representing every state. Ansel wanted to cross over the lagoon to the wooded island, but Casey nudged him in the direction of the giant wheel he could still see sticking up into the sky.

"Let's go down here," he said. They were facing a long thoroughfare called the Midway Plaisance, jutting straight west from the main body of the fair. As soon as they passed under the archway, the whole

feel of the fair changed. The main fair had been filled
with dignified buildings with names like "Manufac-

turing," "Electricity," "Transportation," and "Agriculture," as well as classic statues, lagoons, bridges, and colonnades. The Midway, on the other hand, was an amusement area, filled with sights and sounds from around the world. As the two boys walked down the Midway, they passed Hagenbeck's Animal Show, advertising lions that rode horses and tigers that rode bicycles . . . several show theaters . . . a German Village with clockmakers and bakery . . . and "A Street in Cairo," crowded with fairgoers enjoying the outdoor bazaar, dancing girls, and camel rides.

But Casey only had eyes for the giant wheel in the middle of the Midway. It was even bigger up close than it had seemed earlier. A large sign called it a Ferris Wheel. It had been invented by an American named George Ferris and was 264 feet high, with thirty-six enclosed cars holding forty people each. But it wasn't going around.

Casey noticed a group of workmen tinkering with the giant cogs. "Say!" he called. "We'd like to ride this wheel! Will it be running today?"

"You and a thousand other fairgoers," laughed one of the men. "Sorry . . . it ain't up and running yet. Got a few more kinks to work out. Come back in a few days."

A few days! Casey thought, dismayed. Once circus performances started, they'd never get another chance to get back to the fair!

But a gentleman standing off to the side watching the work ambled over. "Didn't you gents say you were going to give it a spin once you adjusted the speed mechanism?" he asked with the superior tone of a supervisor. "Let these boys go around then. They can be our guinea pigs."

The men laughed. "Yes, sir."

Casey couldn't believe his ears. They were going to get to ride the Ferris Wheel after all!

The man, who must've been the work boss, opened the door to one of the glass cages suspended between the two outer rims of the wheel. Inside were rows of plush seats—forty of them!—facing the windows on all sides. Excited, Ansel and Casey bounced from seat to seat . . . until, all of a sudden, the big wheel started to turn.

The wheel jerked unevenly, causing the car to swing back and forth. The boys held on tight as the boxlike car went back, back, back . . . and then up, up, up. Casey plastered his nose against one of the windows as the ground fell away, and he felt himself lifted high up into the air. His stomach felt like it had dropped into his feet. He looked anxiously at Ansel, but the youngest Eugene's face was flushed with excitement.

As the car curved to the top of the revolution and started with a rush down the other side, the wheel suddenly jerked to a stop with a mighty squeal of metal. The car shuddered and swung back and forth, suspended hundreds of feet in the air.

Terrified, Casey gasped, "What happened? Why did we stop?"

"I don't know," said Ansel, looking worried himself. The boys tried to look out the back windows, down through the maze of metal braces to where the big axel and cogs were connected to the motor, but all they could see were several workmen scurrying about far below them. Spread out before them were the tops of the fair buildings, and beyond them, Lake Michigan. But down below, fairgoers, like so many ants, were gathering in knots on the Midway, pointing at the giant wheel.

Suddenly Casey had a hard time getting a breath. His heart began to beat fast. What if something went wrong . . . what if the car broke loose and they plummeted to the ground? All those people were looking—some looked like they were laughing and having a good time. Didn't they know two boys were stuck up here?

"Are you okay?" Ansel asked as Casey breathed hard. Casey nodded, but couldn't speak. He didn't want Ansel to know he was frightened, but he couldn't get rid of the panicky feeling in his chest. The walls of the car seemed to close in on him; he wished he could open one of the windows and get some fresh air.

It seemed like five minutes dragged by, then ten, then Casey lost all sense of time. He banged on the windows and yelled, "Help! Help! Get us down from here!"

"They can't hear us," Ansel said reasonably. "Don't worry. That man knows we're up here; he'll get us down."

And then, just as suddenly, the machinery groaned and the wheel started to move once more.

Casey squeezed his eyes shut with relief. He opened them once, but suddenly couldn't stand to see the ground rushing up at them. He closed them again, trying to get his breathing back to normal, until the wheel stopped once more, the door to the car was opened, and the supervisor's voice said cheerfully, "Well, now, boys . . . what'd you think of that ride?"

Casey stumbled out of the car and walked away from the Ferris Wheel as rapidly as he could.

"Hey, Casey, wait for me!" Ansel called, running up behind him. "Don't you want to look around some more?"

But Casey just kept walking back the way they had come, his face burning with embarrassment. He had panicked on top of the Ferris Wheel. What if Ansel told Pierre and Raoul? Would they let him go up on the trapeze this afternoon?

Chapter 8

Fall From the Flying Trapeze

"WHERE HAVE YOU BEEN, Casey Watkins?" Eph Thompson demanded when the boys got back to the lot at the corner of Michigan Avenue and Madison Street, where Forepaugh's circus tents were billowing in the strong wind off the lake.

"Handing out circus flyers, whadd'ya think?" Casey said crossly.

"Oh, yeah?" said Eph. "Most of the fellas got back a couple hours ago. We got a performance at two o'clock today, remember? Which means we got elephants to feed and water and harness. Don't wanna

78

send these beasts into the arena mad and hungry, now, do we?"

Casey hurriedly grabbed the water buckets for the grueling process of bringing water to the thirsty animals, which often guzzled thirty to forty gallons a day—each.

"Oh, yeah," Eph called after him. "Pierre Eugene was here a while ago looking for you. Said something about wanting to run through the act one more time before the performance."

Oh, great, Casey groaned, *now everybody's mad at me.* Then he began feeling sorry for himself. This was supposed to be his big day . . . the day he became a circus performer on the flying trapeze! He reminded himself that Eph was feeling bad about not getting to do the John L. Sullivan act. But, still, why did he have to take it out on Casey?

He was so busy with his thoughts that he almost didn't see the stout man and the boy wandering among the animals of Forepaugh's menagerie. Then he realized it was that preacher, Mr. Moody! Was he here to see McCaddon again on business? Or was he actually going to come to the circus, after all?

Casey almost called out to them, until he saw that they were looking at one of McCaddon's new circus flyers—the one that said, "Ha! Ha! Ha! Three Big Shows . . ."

"They're making fun of you, Papa," said the boy in a hurt voice.

"Now, now, it's no big thing, Paul," the big man said, chuckling. " 'He who is not against us is for us.'

Why does it matter *why* people come, just so they come and hear the Word of God being preached."

Casey didn't wait to hear any more but slunk out of sight with his buckets and hurried back to the elephant tent. He didn't want that boy, Paul Moody, asking *him* about why the crazy flyer was making fun of his father. He already had enough troubles today.

Pierre bawled out both boys for not getting back in time for another practice before the opening performance, then hustled them into their costumes and ran them through warm-up exercises to loosen their muscles. Casey was so busy he didn't even have time to see his mother and sister before all the performers lined up for the opening march. Then he saw Cara with the clowns, dressed like a funny, old lady pushing a baby buggy with a big clown in it dressed as an infant!

He laughed and waved at his little sister. *This* was what the circus was all about—making people laugh, helping them forget their troubles, giving them a good show! He took a deep breath, and his sagging spirits rose. He was going to forget all the frustrations of the day and concentrate on what he was supposed to do.

The Eugenes' act didn't come till after intermission, but Casey was too nervous to sit still. After the opening march, he helped Eph line up the elephants in the right order to go back in for their acts. Eph disappeared when Addie Forepaugh took Baby John into the ring for the boxing act, leaving Casey alone on watch with the other elephants. Casey didn't blame him. It was hard to hear the crowd roaring with laughter at the funny act, as "John L. Sullivan" knocked down the famous animal trainer . . . hard knowing it was Eph—not Addie—who had developed that act.

Still, he was glad when Eph came back, and he could change his costume for the 1776 Spectacle. As he and Cara and his mother ran out of the ring after pulling down the statue of King George, leaving the "Redcoats" and "militia" to wage the War of 1776 in the center ring, Doreen gave him a quick hug and said, "You're gonna do great up there, Casey."

Casey barely remembered changing back into his yellow costume . . . coating his hands with resin to keep them from slipping . . . listening to Pierre's last-minute instructions . . . hearing the band strike up a lively number to indicate that intermission was over.

Suddenly it was time!

He heard the ringmaster booming through his megaphone, "Ladies and gentlemen, children of all ages . . . Forepaugh's Circus is proud to present . . . The Eugene Brothers! Masters of the flying trapeze! They will take your breath away as . . ."

Casey walked out with Pierre, Raoul, and Ansel as the clapping of the spectators drowned out the rest of the ringmaster's speech. Pierre went up the far pole, while Raoul and Ansel went up to the near platform. With the band playing lightly in the background, Casey watched from below as Raoul and Pierre did an amazing series of somersaults, spins, and twists in the air, flying back and forth from bar to bar. Then Ansel flew to Pierre and they did a "Flying Angel." Raoul caught the bar and the two older brothers passed Ansel back and forth between them several times.

Finally both Raoul and Ansel came back to the platform as Pierre swung back and forth by his legs from the catcher's bar. As Casey gripped the handholds on the pole and climbed up to the platform, he heard the ringmaster say, "And now, ladies and gentlemen, the young Eugene Twins will do a feat developed especially for the World's Fair here in Chicago . . . the spectacular double pass!"

As Casey stepped onto the platform, he was greeted with thunderous applause from the packed tent. He and Ansel raised their arms in salute to the crowd, as Pierre had taught them. Then Ansel grabbed the fly bar and was gone, swishing smoothly through the air. Before Casey knew it, the bar came back empty, and he realized Ansel was swinging from Pierre's grip on the catcher's bar. Raoul grabbed the bar and handed it to Casey.

A baby cried somewhere; for just a second Casey took his eyes off Ansel and Pierre and looked down. The sea of faces below were all looking up at *him*. His mouth went dry, and his knees started shaking. During practice the seats were empty; if other people were in the rings, they were busy practicing their own acts. Seeing thousands of faces staring up at him unnerved Casey. The ride on the Ferris Wheel that morning flashed through his mind. They'd been trapped so high, so far above the ground. Now here he was far above the ground on the trapeze platform. What if he fell? It wasn't just fun . . . it was *dangerous.*

Suddenly, Casey felt like he couldn't breathe. Unbidden, the same panicky feeling he'd felt on the Ferris Wheel gripped him, and he stood on the platform, frozen.

"You missed your cue!" Raoul hissed in his ear. "Don't look down! Keep your eyes on Pierre!"

Casey shook his head to clear it, tried to get a breath, tried to focus his attention. He heard Raoul's voice in his ear, "Get ready . . . ready . . . GO NOW!"

Casey gripped the bar, jumped up and off the platform, swinging in a long arc toward Pierre and Ansel. Something didn't feel right—he didn't have enough momentum. But in the next swing he was supposed to get his legs over the bar . . . there, he did it . . . but he wasn't swinging out far enough. He needed more time to get a higher swing! But just then he saw Pierre mouth the word, "READY!" He knew that meant that on the next "out swing" Pierre would throw Ansel back toward Casey's bar; Casey was supposed to let go and fly toward Pierre, leaving the bar free for Ansel who would pass him in the air.

He had to let go of the bar or he and Ansel would crash in midair! In desperation, Casey released his legs at the last moment and stretched his arms

83

toward Pierre . . . Ansel came hurtling past him . . . but Casey knew he was going to miss the grip! He felt himself falling toward the net. . . .

At the last second, Casey realized he was falling face forward—the wrong position for a fall! He tried to twist to the side and felt his shoulder slam into the net. The net bounced his body back up into an ungainly flip. This time he came down facing the other way on the back of his head and shoulders. A few more bounces, and Casey lay trembling on the net, aware of the thick ropes biting into his skin.

Everything seemed strangely quiet . . . and then he heard the band strike up "Stars and Stripes Forever"—the circus code that there had been an accident.

Chapter 9

Wanted: Average Talent

L UCKY BOY . . . NO BROKEN BONES," the doctor
drawled to Doreen Watkins, still in her bareback riding costume, who had been hovering anxiously as the circus doctor examined Casey. "Make
sure he rests awhile, Mrs. Watkins. He might be
sore, but he'll be all right."

Casey gritted his teeth and turned his head away.
He almost wished he *had* broken an arm or a leg or
something. *Anything* to divert attention from the
fact that he'd made a fool of himself in front of
thousands of people.

As Casey lay restlessly on the straw pallet in the
Watkins's makeshift dressing room, he could still
hear the excited "oohs" and "ahhs" of the crowd as
the circus performance continued. Later he heard

someone—it sounded like Pierre Eugene—speaking in a low voice to his mother outside the curtain. Casey desperately wanted to know if Ansel had caught the fly bar after the double pass, but he was too humiliated to ask. His first public performance on the trapeze . . . and he had blown it!

Just then he heard heavy footsteps, the curtain was pulled back roughly, and Joe McCaddon stuck his face in. The circus manager glared at Casey for a moment, then dropped the curtain.

"Well, Eugene, looks like it takes more than hair dye to make a fly boy!" Casey heard the man snap angrily. "Your so-called 'Eugene Twin' has embarrassed the whole show!"

Casey's face burned. Well, that was it. He wasn't going to embarrass the whole circus—or himself—again. The Eugene Brothers could just forget the new act. After what happened today, they'd probably be relieved if he quit and saved them the trouble of firing him.

The two o'clock show was finally over. Casey could hear excited children and adults spilling out from the Big Top, hawkers selling souvenirs, and the performers and animals returning to their tents. Frustrated, Casey got up—and winced. The left side of his face stung from a rope burn where he'd hit the safety net, and his left shoulder ached. Otherwise he felt okay.

But what should he do now? He couldn't go outside; everybody was probably laughing at him.

Just then Eph Thompson stuck his head into the

dressing room. "So, you're on your feet. Good!"

Casey said nothing. Why didn't people just leave him alone? But the elephant boss came in and just looked at Casey for few moments. Embarrassed, Casey dropped his eyes.

"Guess today wasn't such a great day for either one of us, eh?" Eph said quietly.

Casey looked up. Yeah . . . Eph understood.

"Well!" said Eph, slapping his wool hat against his leg. "Nothin's gained by moping. C'mon. We gotta get these jungle beasts fed and watered."

Working with Eph turned out to be good medicine. The hard, physical work helped ease some of the tension he felt inside and made him feel useful. Still, he knew the clowns and other performers were talking about him by their sly glances and little snickers. And the roustabout named Tucker was the worst of all.

"Tsk, tsk. The lil' fake Frenchy just couldn't compete under the Big Top with the professionals," the man jeered as Casey was refilling his buckets at the water barrels. "Had himself a fally-wally."

Casey seethed inside but said nothing. His mother had said this would all blow over in a few days. Maybe so . . . but he wasn't going to give people like Tucker another chance to make fun of him.

By the time the crowds were pushing and shoving

for tickets that evening, Casey had convinced himself that the Eugene brothers wouldn't want him to try the act again, so he was surprised when Pierre stopped by the Watkins's dressing room just before the eight o'clock show.

The Frenchman looked at him . . . hard. "So. Are you going up on the trapeze tonight?" he asked abruptly.

"B-but . . . I . . . I thought . . ." Casey stammered.

"I don't care what you thought. I'm asking, are you going up tonight?"

Casey just stared at him.

"Look, Watkins," Pierre said. "I'm not going to beg you or try to convince you. I just want to know yes or no."

"My mother doesn't want me to do the act anymore," Casey hedged. It was true in a way; she'd never been happy about it, and he knew the fall had frightened her.

"You're right, she doesn't," Pierre agreed. "But I already talked to your mother. She's willing to leave the decision up to you."

Casey was confused. Did the Eugenes still want to take a chance on him? For a brief moment he felt flattered, wanted to . . . but then he remembered the terrible humiliation of falling—failing!—in front of thousands of spectators. What if it happened again? He'd never live it down.

"No," he said, staring at the ground.

There was no reply. When Casey looked up, Pierre was gone.

❖ ❖ ❖ ❖

Doreen Watkins insisted that Casey participate as usual in the opening march, parading the elephants with Eph, and then doing his small bit in the 1776 Spectacle. But after the intermission, as he was standing behind the tent flap, he heard the ringmaster announce dramatically, "The Eugene Brothers, on the flying trapeze!" He couldn't bear to stick around and hear any more.

After changing out of his 1776 costume, Casey walked quickly away from the circus tents. In a short time, the huge department stores and office buildings of Chicago had swallowed up the sounds of the circus along the lakefront. Dusk had finally fallen, and he walked along the darkening streets, hands jammed in his trouser pockets. Carriages with smartly dressed men and women clipped past him, out on the town on a warm Saturday night. He passed several bars churning out rowdy laughter and music, small cafes and fancy restaurants, brightly lit theaters—all full of people having a good time. But Casey barely noticed. All he could think about was how miserable he felt.

It just wasn't fair! God—if there was a God—had really handed him a raw deal. His father had been killed, which turned Casey's whole life upside down. The months in Philadelphia had been miserable. He'd thought the circus would give him and Mama and Cara a new start on life . . . but the circus was no different than anywhere else. Everybody was just out for themselves. And even though his mother

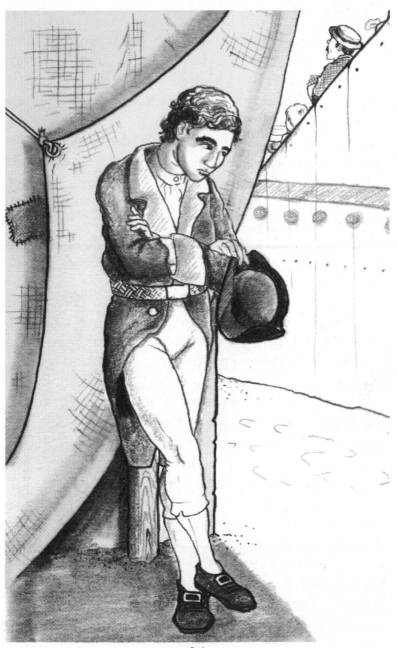

enjoyed riding the circus horses, he knew she wasn't really happy. Life in a railroad car wasn't a home. She had kids to raise, but being a single woman now—a pretty one at that—she had to work hard just to avoid the unwanted attention of men on the road who wanted to fool around.

His emotions churning, Casey absently turned a corner and headed down a different street. He was the man of the family now. He should have been taking care of his mother and sister. But he'd been so eager to become a circus star that he hardly paid any attention to them. And now look where it'd gotten him. He was a failure—the laughingstock of the circus. He'd let everybody down.

Tears stung Casey's eyes. Maybe it was just as well his father was dead. At least he didn't have to see disappointment written on his father's face.

Casey hadn't been paying much attention to what streets he'd turned on or how far he'd walked. But as he passed an alley he became aware of a group of young people—boys and girls about his age—jostling each other down some narrow stairs into a meeting hall in the basement of a large building. Young men in their twenties stood on the sidewalk calling out, "Come on in to Moody's Youth Meeting! . . . Everybody's welcome! . . . Come on in! Be part of God's movement going on all over this great city!"

The name caught Casey's attention. Moody? Wasn't that the same man who'd rented the circus tent for a preaching service tomorrow? He hesitated . . . but decided he didn't feel like mingling with a bunch of strangers. Then an enthusiastic young man grabbed Casey by the arm and said, "Come on in! There's plenty of room. Moody himself is going to be here a little later."

Casey started to protest but found himself being cheerfully propelled down the stairs and into the basement hall. Rows of chairs were filled with young people chatting gaily with one other—boys playfully horsing around on one side of the room, the girls eyeing them and whispering behind their hands on the other. A couple girls smiled at Casey, so he decided to sit down in the back row and see what this "youth meeting" was all about.

Someone began playing a piano, and one of the men led the youthful crowd in singing hymn after hymn. Casey didn't know the words, although he recognized some of the tunes from Uncle John's church services back in Philadelphia. But in Uncle John's church, all the hymns sounded mournful, like funeral dirges; here the singing was loud and spirited.

During the singing there was a commotion at the door, and Mr. Moody came bustling in, with his son Paul right behind him. Casey slouched down in his chair; he didn't want them to recognize him, because he suddenly had a horrible thought: Mr. Moody and his son had probably been at the circus that afternoon and seen him bungle his act! Casey looked around, thinking it was a good time to leave . . . but just then the room quieted, and Mr. Moody stood up to speak.

"There's nothin' I like better than a room full of young people singin' praises to God," the man boomed, a wide smile on his whiskered face. "You young people in Chicago sing *almost* as well as the girls and boys at my schools in Massachusetts." He grinned. "Maybe the next time we have a youth conference at Northfield Girls School or Mt. Hermon Boys School, all you Chicago young people oughta come and we'll have a singin' contest. How 'bout it?"

The room erupted with cheers and hollering.

Moody raised his arms for quiet before he continued. "Now all of you know that Chicago is hostin' a grand event this summer . . . the World's Columbian Exposition . . . six months of celebrating mankind's achievements durin' the past century."

Heads nodded and the young people murmured to one another.

"But what the world don't realize is that *another* grand event is happenin' in Chicago this summer! At this very moment there are several evangelistic services goin' on all over this city with speakers from round the world. This past week we have held women's meetin's, children's meetin's, meetin's for sailors and soldiers, meetin's in the jails, meetin's for Germans, Poles, Bohemians, Jews, and Arabs in their native tongues on the fairgrounds . . . even meetin's on the streets late at night for the drunks and the prostitutes!"

Casey smiled as the room burst out laughing. He'd forgotten about trying to sneak out.

"Do ya know why? I'll tell ya why. When I was the

age of you young people, I was an ambitious fella. I wanted ta sell shoes. An' I did. Ain't no exaggeration that I was the best shoe salesman this side of the Mississippi."

More laughter.

"I was a religious fella, too. Brought hundreds of children and young people to Sunday school every Sunday. Used to ride my horse Paint round the streets, give rides to as many younguns as could hang on, and herded the rest to the church."

This time Moody joined the laughter. But then his voice changed.

"And then somethin' happened that changed my life. One of the Sunday school teachers was dyin' of lung disease. An' he was concerned because none of the girls in his class were Christians. So he asked me to go round with him to each home and talk personally to each girl. Well . . . ya could say I was kinda uncomfortable. Wasn't convertin' people a job for ordained ministers and deacons? But I went.

"These were not well-to-do girls. These were girls from the slums, right here in Chicago. Their homes were small and miserable. But ya know what? Each and every girl in that class gave her heart to Jesus. Broken lives were changed! And all because one man was concerned about their souls!"

The room was hushed, the young crowd listening.

"An' I tell you," Moody said, shaking a finger at the faces in front of him, "it changed my life. What was sellin' shoes, when I could be sellin' the Gospel? What did it matter if I made one thousand or even ten thousand dollars, when I could be winning one thousand or even ten thousand souls for Christ!"

Spontaneously, the young people clapped. Moody waited until the enthusiastic crowd had settled down and then said, "Now, most of ya can tell I ain't had much education by the way I speak." A few titters rippled around the room. "But it just goes to prove that God can use ordinary people to do His work—the most important work in the world. And that's what I wanna tell you young people tonight.

"If this world is gonna be reached for Christ, it's gotta be done by men and women of *average talent.* After all, there are comparatively few people in the world who have great talent! How many Thomas Edisons are there? How many Alexander Graham Bells? How many Charles Dickenses? I'm here to tell ya . . . not many. But it doesn't take an Edison or a Bell or a Dickens to care about a lost soul. All it takes is love for that lost soul, and the willingness to stand there in the gap between heaven and hell, inviting that lost soul to accept God's free gift of salvation for all eternity."

The room was so quiet, it seemed as if everyone had stopped breathing.

"We need gap men and gap women—like these folks helpin' ta lead this meetin' tonight, young people studyin' the Bible at the Chicago Bible Institute, a school that's only four years old. You don't have to be a great preacher, goin' all over the world like I do. You don't have ta be the pastor of a large church. All ya have ta do is be willin' to give your life to God to use in whatever way He wants ta use you. Bow your heads now. I want to pray an' . . ."

The meeting seemed like it was coming to an end. Suddenly Casey remembered that he better get out of there before Mr. Moody or his son realized who he was. As the boys and girls around him bowed their heads, he got up quietly and slipped out the door and up the stairs to the street. But as his footsteps echoed on the pavement heading back toward the lakefront, they seemed to echo Mr. Moody's words . . .

"It's the most important work in the world . . . need men and women of average talent to stand in the gap . . . gap men and gap women. . . ."

Chapter 10

Moody's Show

THE SECOND SHOW WAS OVER when Casey got back to the circus, and his mother was pacing back and forth in front of their small, curtained sleeping quarters.

"Where have you been, Casey Watkins!" she said angrily. "You gave me a scare!"

"I . . . I'm sorry, Mama. I just couldn't hang around . . . I was out walkin'."

"In a strange city? As big as Chicago? Anything could've happened!" Doreen said, close to tears.

Casey's guilty feelings came rushing back. The last person he wanted to hurt was his mother . . . but it looked as though everything he did came up wrong.

"Just went to a youth meetin' where that Mr. Moody preached—kinda stumbled on it by accident.

Besides, I'm fourteen, Mama," he said defensively. "I can take care of mysel—"

Casey stopped. That sounded pretty hollow after falling from the trapeze today. It was useless to argue. Freezing his face into a mask, he threw himself down on his straw pallet and turned his face away.

❖ ❖ ❖ ❖

The next morning—Sunday—he got up while his mother and Cara were still asleep and, feeling like he had to do *something* with himself, went to help Eph do chores as usual. He was exercising Queen Victoria, walking the big elephant briskly around the circus lot to avoid having to talk to anybody, when he saw Mr. Moody standing outside the main tent talking to Joe McCaddon. It was only eight o'clock; Moody's service wasn't until ten. What was the preacher doing here so early?

"Whatsa matter, Moody?" McCaddon was saying, chomping on an unlit cigar. "Gettin' cold feet? Forepaugh's show had almost a full house last night—that's ten thousand people. Think you can top that? Ha, ha!"

"He'll be lucky to get three thousand!" laughed one of the roustabouts lounging nearby. "Whoever heard of holdin' church in a circus tent?"

"Ya heard of it now!" said Moody, chuckling. "Guess ya'll just have to come an' see, won't ya? But right now, Mr. McCaddon, I've come to ask a small favor. We need help gettin' some of the circus equipment out of the way so we can set up a simple platform in the middle of the . . . er, performing area."

"Humph! That wasn't part of the contract," Joe McCaddon grumbled. Nevertheless, he yelled, "Hey, Tucker! Wilson! Get about ten men and help the preacher here clear an area for his platform!"

Casey moved on with the big elephant, but as soon as his chores were done, he hurried back to the dressing room. "We're going to go to church today, Casey!" Cara said, jumping up and down with excitement. "Right here in the circus tent! An' I'm gonna wear a dress!"

Casey looked quizzically at his mother. "You, Mama? You're not much of a churchgoer." He remembered going to a Catholic church on Christmas and Easter when he was younger, but he never understood any of the words because everything was in Latin . . . and of course, they all went to Uncle John's Protestant church in Philadelphia as part of "the deal"—but that was only for a few months. Cara was the only one who seemed to like it, and that was because she got to go with her cousin Elspeth to Sunday school.

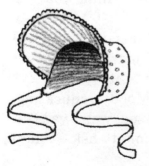

"Well," his mother said, setting a bonnet—fashionable a few years earlier—on her thick, red hair and stabbing a hatpin through it, "maybe I shoulda gone more often. Besides, you said you 'accidentally' heard this Mr. Moody preach last night. Now it's my turn. He's a very famous preacher, you know." She turned around, showing off the pretty, summer dress that hung to her ankles. "How do I look?"

"Beautiful!" said Cara, still bouncing.

"Coming Casey?" said Doreen Watkins, as she and Cara prepared to leave.

Casey frowned. He'd kinda like to hear Mr. Moody speak again—that youth meeting last night wasn't anything like Uncle John's church services! but he dreaded running into Ansel or the other Eugene brothers . . . or other people who might think he was a coward for not going up on the trapeze with the Eugene Brothers last night.

"Nah, guess not," he said, faking a yawn. "I'm pretty tired."

But fifteen minutes after his mother and sister had left, Casey was bored. This was ridiculous! He couldn't stay cooped up in this dressing room the rest of his life. He'd just have to go out and face the music. After all, he had his reasons for quitting. Still, as Casey picked his way through the animal tents, parade wagons, and circus equipment, he did his best to avoid actually talking to anybody.

He passed a bunch of the clowns—without their corny costumes and clown makeup—talking about whether they should go to "Moody's show" or not.

"I say let's go," said one, whose circus name was Cedric the Cop. "I ain't been in a church for . . . maybe fifteen years. And now it's come to us, right in our laps! It'll be good for a laugh anyway."

"Hey, yeah!" agreed another. "Maybe we can steal some of Moody's speech and work it into our act!"

That idea was greeted with a great deal of guffawing, and the clowns sauntered off in the direction of the Big Top.

Casey waited until he heard singing in the tent, then slipped inside. His mouth dropped open; he could hardly believe his eyes. Not only were all ten thousand of the regular seats filled, but rows and rows of extra chairs and benches had been set up in the center area, along with a large, wooden platform in the middle—all filled with people. Why, Casey figured, there must be *eighteen thousand people* in the tent!

The song leader, a distinguished-looking man with a white moustache and mutton chop whiskers, led the huge crowd in singing hymns and several times sang a solo, his incredible voice reaching the last rows of the huge tent. Then a large choir crowded onto the platform and sang several songs. In between songs a few people got up and told something they called "testimonies"—stories about how God saved them and turned their lives around.

Casey kept inching his way closer to the platform so he could hear better. The words of one hymn seemed to ring over and over . . .

Nearer, my God, to Thee,
Nearer to Thee!
E'en tho it be a cross
That raiseth me;

Still all my song shall be,
Nearer, my God, to Thee,
Nearer, my God, to Thee,
Nearer to Thee!

As the words "Nearer to Thee" seemed to hang in the great tent, Mr. Moody got up to speak.

"Thank you, Mr. Sankey, for leadin' us in that beautiful worship," he said, his voice booming clearly. "I want to tell you good folks that last year that there song came to mean a great deal to me. My doctor had recently told me I had ta slow down, spend less time workin' and more time restin'. Shortly after that I was returnin' home from meetin's in England and Ireland with my oldest son, Will, on the ocean liner *Spree*, when there was an accident at sea.

"All the passengers spent a couple terrifyin' nights gathered together in the ship's salon, not knowing whether the ship would sink before we were rescued. We took comfort from reading Scripture and singing great hymns like the one we just finished . . . 'Nearer, my God, to Thee, Nearer to Thee'."

Moody had everyone's attention—even, Casey noticed, the circus clowns and roustabouts who were leaning against some of the poles and rigging.

"But I have ta tell ya, that there situation posed a dilemma for me," Moody went on. "I realized I might well die right there in the middle of the ocean. Now, I ain't afraid of dyin'. But it made me mad. It seemed like there was still a lot of work to do bringin' the Good News to a lost world. So I told God if He chose

to bring us safely home, I wasn't goin' to waste any
time restin' as long as I had any strength and He had

work for me ta do."

Moody looked around at the masses of people surrounding him on every side. "Well," he chuckled, "seein' as how I'm standin' up here today, I guess ya all can figure out the rest of the story."

Appreciative laughter rippled through the tent.

Moody's voice rose. "I think God decided it wasn't time ta take this ol' body home yet, 'cause someone in this tent today doesn't know that God loves you!" He waved his Bible in the air. "It's here in this here book . . . but some of you haven't looked in here for a while." He flipped open some pages. "'For God so loved the world,'" he read, "'that He gave His only begotten Son . . . that whosoever believeth in Him, should not perish'—*should not perish, my friends!*— 'but have everlastin' life.'"

Casey was amazed. This Mr. Moody was a preacher, all right . . . but what was this about Go loving everybody? When Uncle John preached, always ranted about how evil the world was, a people didn't mend their ways, God was goi send them all to hell. In general, it had seemed to Casey like God was mad at ev looking for a good excuse to punish people

But Mr. Moody went on and on, tal how God loved the world so much that Son Jesus to take the punishment for e

Casey frowned. He wasn't so sur God loved him so much, why did ev be going so wrong for him?

Chapter 11

No Room for Quitters

ON WAS IN A ROTTEN MOOD on Monday.
Moody's "show" filled the tent to
orning, but Forepaugh's two
d evening had been poorly

see the day when
The Greatest
ng. "That's
o much

nself if he
right now he
Two days had
adn't even talked
d to; in fact, he was

d
He
d if
ng to
always
rybody,
king about
He sent His
erybody's sin.
about this. If
e about this. If
rything seem to

doing his best to avoid everybody except his mother and Eph Thompson. Still . . . he wondered why Ansel hadn't come by to see him. Was he blaming Casey for blowing the act on Saturday? Obviously he was, or he would've come by. This made Casey angry. He'd thought Ansel was a better friend than that. Now he knew the truth; the Eugene brothers had just been using him to spice up their act with a new trick. They didn't care about him. Not even Ansel.

As Eph trimmed the elephants' toenails, Casey sat on an upturned bucket in the elephant quarters staring moodily at the hard-packed ground. He felt trapped. He didn't want to stay with the circus any longer. He didn't want to leave Eph in the lurch, but the tension he felt was unbearable. He couldn't imagine going on this way for five more months on the road, with people making fun of him . . . or ignoring him.

But the season didn't end until October. What about his mother and sister? He couldn't just leave them. And where would he go? What would he do?

Casey's jumbled thoughts were interrupted as Eph kicked over another bucket and sat on it, facing him. "Want to talk about it?" he asked.

Casey just shrugged his shoulders.

"Your mind made up about not doing the act?"

"Whadd'ya think?" Casey muttered.

"How come?" Eph pressed.

Casey snorted. "Pretty obvious, ain't it? I can't do it."

"You did it before Saturday."

"Yeah, well . . . that was during practice. It's different up there when the pressure's on." Casey's mouth twitched involuntarily as he remembered the panicky feeling he felt at the top of the Ferris Wheel . . . and again on the platform in front of all those people.

"I think you oughta give it another try," said Eph.

Casey stood up angrily. "Yeah, well, what you think doesn't really count much in this business, does it, Eph?"

The moment the words came out of his mouth, Casey knew they were cruel. Eph was still hurting from losing his popular boxing act to Addie Forepaugh; the comment was mean to rub it in. He wanted to say he was sorry, but the elephant boss had already risen abruptly and gone back to trimming toenails.

Feeling even worse, Casey walked out of the elephant tent . . . and just kept walking.

It was high noon, and the hot, humid weather was only slightly helped by the constant breeze off the lake. The Chicago streets were full of business people, shoppers, sightseers, fancy carriages with high-stepping horses, and dray horses pulling heavy loads. After dodging the heavy traffic awhile, Casey saw a familiar wagon—the Bible Institute wagon Moody had been driving when the circus parade had passed by. Suddenly Casey had an urge to talk to the big man. He seemed like a friendly sort—not likely to turn a boy away. He wasn't connected with the circus—except for renting the tent. And besides that,

Casey liked the way he'd talked to the boys and girls at the youth meeting. Mr. Moody had made a big point about God using people of "average talent" to do important things.

It was pretty obvious to Casey that he fell into that category. Casey Watkins: Average Talent. But maybe Mr. Moody would have some ideas of what he could do if he left the circus. He'd talked about needing "gap men" and "gap women" . . . what did that mean? Maybe he could use Casey!

Excited, Casey ran up to the wagon. A service was going on, right there on the sidewalk. Two young men and a woman were singing a hymn, while four or five passersby stood listening. But he didn't see Mr. Moody.

A couple workingmen came by and heckled the little group, making rude comments. If that happened in the circus, Casey knew, there'd be a fight in two seconds. But the Bible Institute students just called out, "Come listen for a few minutes. We have some Good News for you." When the hecklers just laughed and started to pass on, one of the young men went running after them. "At least take these Gospels of John and read them. Go ahead, they're free."

When the young man came back, Casey got his attention. "Is Mr. Moody here?" he asked.

"No," said the young man, "he's leading meetings somewhere else in the city."

Casey felt keenly disappointed. "Do you know when he'll be back in this part of town?"

"Well, tonight actually. He takes a turn going out

with the wagon and speaking on the street. You could try to find him then. But . . ." The young man hesitated. "I'd be careful, if I were you. It can get kinda rough after dark."

✧ ✧ ✧ ✧

Casey left the circus right after intermission of the evening show and headed back into the city. At least McCaddon ought to feel better, he thought. The Monday crowds had perked up again and filled the tent for both shows. Maybe the Sunday thing was just a quirk.

It was late, going on ten o'clock. The streets still bustled with activity, but the people had changed. The fancy carriage horses still clipped briskly down the streets, but on the sidewalks he saw more ordinary people lounging about, trying to escape the day's heat. As he moved away from the downtown stores and office buildings, he saw drunks sprawled in doorways and ladies with painted faces flirting with strange men who passed by.

He walked quickly, remembering the young man's warning. But after walking fruitlessly up one street and down the next, he thought he wasn't going to find the Bible Institute wagon.

And then he saw it. Even from a block away he could hear Mr. Moody's voice and see his distinctive shape standing on the seat of the hearselike wagon. A rather boistrous crowd had gathered in front of a popular saloon to hear the famous preacher. As Casey pushed through the crowd, he noticed some of the roustabouts from the circus standing off to one side, grinning and poking each other. *What are they doing here?* he wondered uneasily.

Mr. Moody was talking to the sidewalk crowd with as much warmth, humor, and zest as the circus-tent crowd yesterday. But as Casey listened, he noticed something strange. The wagon was starting to rock . . . slightly at first, so you'd barely notice it, except that Mr. Moody had to shift his legs to keep his balance. Then the wagon began rocking more; Mr. Moody just took a firm grip on an iron handhold and kept on preaching.

The circus roustabouts were laughing uproariously by this time. Suspicious, Casey bent down and looked under the wagon. A large man was lying on his back under the wagon, rocking it with his legs. At that point the rocking became so severe it seemed as if the wagon was in danger of tipping over, and the normally gentle team of horses were snorting anxiously. Mr. Moody swung off the wagon seat with a grunt as several listeners—angry that anyone should be so disrespectful to a "man of the cloth"—hauled the jokester out from under the wagon.

Casey's eyes bugged. It was Tucker, the bully from the circus!

"Find a copper!" someone yelled from the crowd. "Throw the bum in jail!"

"Yeah! Twelve hours in the slammer might teach 'im some manners."

"Yeah!" Casey yelled. "Lock him up!" He'd like

nothing better than getting Tucker out of his hair and away from his mother. He noticed that the other roustabouts had slunk away when Tucker had been discovered.

"Now, now, now," said Moody, trying to calm the crowd. "We don't need a policeman." He looked Tucker in the eye. "You've had your little joke, sir," Moody said. "Now you owe me fifteen minutes of your time to hear my little talk."

The sneer deepened on Tucker's face as he struggled to loosen his arms. "Why would I wanna do that?" he said scornfully.

"Let him go, my good friends," said Mr. Moody to the helpful bystanders, who reluctantly let go of the bully's arms. "God don't never force anyone . . . though this man would be a fool to not hear what I have to say."

"Fool? Whadd'ya mean?" growled Tucker, trying to look tough again.

"Can't tell ya, 'less ya listen," Mr. Moody said.

Tucker looked around and realized his "pals" had disappeared. "Well," he said with a shrug, "guess it can't hurt to listen for a few minutes."

Mr. Moody began telling a story about a wise man who built a house on solid ground, sinking the foundation into the rock. "This man had a friend," Moody said, "a foolish fellow, who also built a house. But digging into the rock looked like hard work, so he built it quickly on sandy ground. Then the foolish fellow sat back, with his feet up, and laughed at his friend who was still building his house on the rock."

The sidewalk crowd fell silent as Moody continued his story. "No sooner were both houses finished,"

he said, "than a great storm came up. Gale winds blew, rain beat down in torrents, rivers flooded . . . and the house of the man who had foolishly built on the sand crumbled like paper. But the house of the wise man stood strong on the rock."

Listening, Casey frowned. What did the story mean?

"You, sir," Moody said, wagging a finger in Tucker's face, "are like that there foolish man, buildin' your life on things that don't matter. One day the storms of life will come, and the things you've done will crumble into nothing. Even your so-called friends will disappear, just like your buddies did tonight. But," he said, laying a hand on the man's shoulder, "it's not too late to choose a different foundation. I'm talkin' 'bout the foundation of Jesus Christ, the only cornerstone worth buildin' on."

Moody went on talking to the man, as if no one else was standing around looking on. Then, to Casey's astonishment, the man knelt down, right there on the sidewalk, and the two men prayed together! Tucker's shoulders shook with silent sobs as Moody prayed for his soul. *Boy*, Casey thought, *Tucker's putting on a pretty good act.*

When they got to their feet, the two men shook hands vigorously and Tucker walked away into the night. The bold swagger was gone from his walk.

As the crowd melted away, Moody spoke a few words to his Bible school assistants, who then picked up the reins of the horses and drove the wagon away. Left standing on the sidewalk, Moody mopped his face with his handkerchief, took off his coat, and

114

headed down the street on foot.

Instantly Casey ran after him. This was his chance to talk to Moody! As he fell into step with the portly man, he blurted out, "Mr. Moody! Maybe you don't remember me, but . . ."

Mr. Moody stooped abruptly and peered at Casey's face under a streetlamp. A grin broke his face. "Why, sure I do! You're the young fella from the circus! Say, sorry about that fall. Glad to see you weren't badly hurt."

Casey reddened. So, Moody *had* been there and seen him fall. Well, maybe it was just as well. Now the preacher might understand that he wasn't cut out for circus life.

"Well, I, uh . . . see, I came to your show on Sunday, and—"

"Good for you!" boomed Moody, walking again. "I like a young man who keeps a bargain."

"Well, uh, sir . . . I also happened to be at the youth meeting where you spoke Saturday night," Casey rushed on. "You talked to the young people about becoming gap men and gap women in your, uh, work. And . . . well, I'd like to know what someone has to do to become one of your gap men."

"Hmm," said Moody, mopping his forehead once more with his handkerchief. The June night was warm and muggy. "Are you a believer, son?"

"Well, sure . . . I mean, I guess. I mean, I'd like to be," Casey stumbled. He wasn't sure what the right answer was to such a question.

"Hmm," Moody said thoughtfully. "What about

your brothers? You have family in the circus, don't you?"

Casey evaded the question by telling part of the truth. "The Eugene Brothers aren't my real brothers—that's just for show. See?" He pointed to his hair, where telltale red roots could be seen beneath the black dye. "And . . . well, lately I've been thinkin' maybe circus life isn't for me. I've been watching the Bible school students who help you with your meetings, and the Bible wagon and all . . . I think I'd like doin' that."

There. It was out. Would Mr. Moody give him a chance? It was his only hope of getting away from the circus!

"Hmm," the preacher said again. The pair walked along in silence for almost a whole block. Then Moody stopped and looked at Casey in the dim light of the streetlamps. "Just one thing . . . have you been back up on that trapeze?"

Casey hung his head, then shook it slightly.

"I see. Son, there ain't no room among my gap men for quitters. The Christian life is tough! You gotta go to school; you gotta be trained. It's hard work. People might laugh at you, or give you a hard time. Look what happened tonight. A body can't cut and run when the goin' gets tough." Moody laid a fatherly hand on the boy's shoulder. Now, this is my advice . . . you go back up that rope ladder and do your stuff on the flying trapeze. *Then* we'll talk about you becoming one of my gap men."

Casey's disappointment was cut short by a flush

of anger. What did Mr. Moody know about the panic he felt up there on that platform? Casey would like to see *him* up there, see if he could take his own advice.

Caught up in his own thoughts, Casey didn't notice the figures that stepped out from a dark alley and blocked the sidewalk until Moody stopped short. Startled, Casey looked up and froze. A gang of five street toughs were standing in their path, cigarettes dangling from their lips, eyes narrowed, mocking smiles on their faces.

For a moment no one spoke. Then Mr. Moody walked right up to the one who seemed to be the leader and held out his coat. "Would you be so kind, young man, as to hold my coat while I put it on?" He turned to another and held out his Bible. "And you, sir, would you hold my Bible for me?"

Caught off guard, the two young men found themselves holding Mr. Moody's coat and Bible. Keeping up a running commentary about the unpleasant, muggy weather even at this late hour, the graying preacher turned his back and slipped both arms into the arms of the coat. Then, taking back his Bible, he gave a little bow to the surprised young men. "Thank you, good sirs. I hope someone will be as kind to you when you get old."

Then, turning to Casey, he said, "Come along, son."

Astonished, the little gang parted and let Moody and Casey walk past.

A short while later, as Casey watched Mr. Moody swing on board a streetcar with a friendly wave goodbye, his anger was forgotten. That was the bravest thing he'd ever seen, he thought. But . . . the most amazing thing was, Mr. Moody had actually treated those hoodlums with respect, like they were real human beings.

Just like he'd treated that creep Tucker.

Chapter 12

Lost . . .

CASEY TOSSED AND TURNED all night. Finally he gave up trying to sleep and was already hard at work shoveling away dirty straw and manure in the elephant quarters by the time Eph Thompson showed up the next morning.

"Eph?" Casey said quickly, wiping his dirty hands on a rag. "I gotta talk to you."

"Oh, yeah?" said Eph curtly. "Thought my opinion didn't count for much. Remember?"

Casey nodded miserably. "I . . . I'm really sorry, Eph. I was upset and shot off my mouth. I didn't mean it. Fact is, Eph, you're the only real friend I've got. And I

really need to talk to you."

"Humph," Eph said, sticking a straw in his mouth and chewing it suspiciously. "So . . . talk."

Casey grinned. Eph was a brick! "Well," he said nervously, "what you said yesterday about going back up on the trapeze . . . I've been thinkin' it over, and you're right. I oughta at least try. The problem is, the Eugene brothers are really mad at me—at least, Ansel hasn't spoken a word to me since I fell. And I turned Pierre down when he gave me a chance to go up again Saturday night."

Eph's eyebrows went up.

"Yeah, I know," Casey sighed. "Why *should* they give me another chance."

"You got that right," Eph said. "Frankly, Casey Watkins, you've been acting like a wounded polecat, unloadin' your stinkin' attitude on anybody who gets close. By all rights, you don't *deserve* another chance. But," he added, plucking the straw from his mouth and waving it at Casey, "you want my advice? There's only one way to find out for sure. Swallow your pride and go ask 'em. You sure ain't got nothin' to lose."

✧ ✧ ✧ ✧

Eph was right, Casey decided. If the Eugene brothers were still mad at him . . . if they said no . . . why, that wasn't any different than the way it was now. But if they said yes . . .

Still, that slim hope didn't keep his knees from knocking as he walked into the ring and looked up to

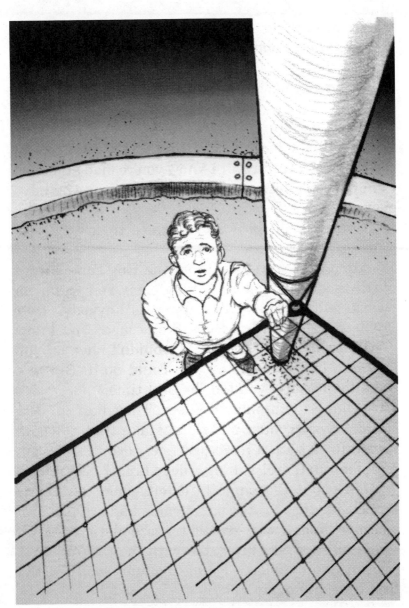

where the three Eugene brothers were warming up
for the afternoon show. Ansel looked down at him

first and stared in surprise . . . then glanced quickly at Pierre and Raoul, as if wanting a cue for how to react.

"What do you want, Watkins?" Pierre called down coolly.

"I . . . I want to try again." Casey pushed the words past the lump in his throat. "I know I ruined the act last Saturday . . . I know you're mad at me . . . I know I don't deserve another chance, and you have every right to—"

"Shut up and give us a chance to come down, Watkins," Pierre said.

When they were seated on the ring curb, Pierre continued, "Let's get one thing clear. Your problem wasn't falling. That can happen to anybody. Your problem was quitting. Sure, we're mad. You know why? Because you can do it. I wouldn't have let you up there if I didn't think you could do it. But you quit, just because you fell the first time."

"B-but . . ." stammered Casey. They didn't understand. It wasn't just a little mistake that he could brush up on with a little practice. He'd been frozen with fear up there! Taking a deep breath, he tried to explain about the panic he'd felt when the Ferris Wheel got stuck . . . the same panic had gripped him again when he got up on the trapeze platform.

Raoul snorted. "Fear goes with the job, Watkins. Learning to fly means facing the fear—not just the first time, but again and again."

But Pierre looked thoughtful as he turned to his brother. "This panic the boy felt—I partly blame myself. We practiced the routine, but we never practiced getting the boy used to performing in front of a crowd." He stood up and began pacing slowly back and forth, running a hand through his dark hair. "Yes, that is what we must do. Get the boy used to performing in front of a crowd . . . *before* we do the double pass."

Bewildered, Casey looked from Raoul to Ansel to Pierre. "You mean—?"

Pierre grunted. "Yes. You can go up again . . . but we won't start out with the double pass. In fact, the two o'clock performance is as good a time as any to start with something simple."

"*Today?*" Casey gulped.

"What about McCaddon?" Raoul asked his brother.

"Humph," said Pierre. "We'll just do it. We'll worry about McCaddon later."

Ansel's anxious face relaxed into a grin. "But if we're going to be the Eugene Twins again," he said, poking Casey, "that red hair needs a new dye job!"

✧ ✧ ✧ ✧

The plan was simple. The Eugene Brothers' act would go on as usual, with Casey up on the platform so he'd have plenty of time to get used to the height and the crowd. But at the end of the brothers' act, he would swing out on the fly bar, hook his legs and swing upside down, then do a single somersault into the net.

Casey didn't tell anyone—not even his mother—that he was going to try again. He felt a little embarrassed by how simple his routine was . . . a "baby" act. But when he followed Raoul and Ansel onto the platform during the afternoon show and saw the gawking crowd below, the same panic threatened to overwhelm him. What if he froze up and couldn't even do the "baby" act? What if he humiliated himself again?

"Relax, Casey," Raoul said. "There's plenty of time. You can do it."

By the time the Eugene Brothers' act was almost over, he felt a little easier. Ansel went down into the net first, throwing a double somersault on the way. Then Casey went out on the swing . . . and into the net with a single somersault, just like they'd planned. Raoul and Pierre followed, throwing in a few fancy spins on the way down.

As the four "brothers" came running out of the ring, Casey felt almost giddy with relief. He hadn't done much, but at least he'd gone up again. Then he saw that Tucker had been watching the show from the performers' entrance. The boy braced himself for a sarcastic jibe about his "baby" act. He nearly fell over when the burly roustabout just said, "Good goin', Watkins."

✧ ✧ ✧ ✧

McCaddon yelled that it was stupid to put Casey up on the bars again, but somehow Pierre convinced the circus manager it didn't hurt anything to give the boy a simple part. Pierre kept it simple, too. For three days—Tuesday, Wednesday, and Thursday—Casey did nothing but the "baby" act at each performance. Even so, Casey had to fight back the panic each time he stepped out onto the platform.

But in between performances, Pierre had Casey practice the "hocks off" routine where Casey "flew" to Pierre's outstretched hands, but without doing the double pass. At the Friday and Saturday performances, Pierre put Casey's "hocks off" routine into the Eugene Brothers' act . . . and began practicing the double pass between shows.

"I don't like it, Casey," Doreen Watkins fretted. "The double pass seems too dangerous. Falling into the net is one thing . . . but what if you and Ansel collide in the air?"

Casey couldn't reassure his mother; his stomach was a knot of fear every time they practiced the act. "But I can't quit now, Mama," he pleaded. "Even Mr. Moody told me to go back up on the trapeze again. I'm not even sure it's gonna happen. Tomorrow is our last day in Chicago. Pierre might just let it go."

It was true. Pierre hadn't said anything about trying to do the double pass before the circus left Chicago. Still, after the last Saturday performance, he ran Casey and Ansel through another practice.

It was late when Casey walked back toward the Watkins's dressing room. Part of him wished he had a chance to redeem himself by doing the double pass before they left Chicago, and part of him hoped Pierre

125

would forget it. Things were okay now. He was getting used to the crowds, and he'd only missed Pierre's grip once on the "hocks off" routine. Maybe it was best to leave things the way they were.

Just then he heard Tucker's rumbly voice and saw the big roustabout standing outside the curtained dressing room talking to his mother. Adrenalin shot into Casey's tired body. If that big lout was bothering his mother again, he'd—

But by the time Casey ran up to his mother, Tucker had ambled off into the darkness. "Now that was strange," Doreen Watkins murmured.

"What, Mama?" Casey demanded. "Was that man bothering you again?"

"No . . . in fact, he came by to *apologize* for his past behavior. Said I was a real lady, and he would leave me alone from now on. When I expressed surprise at his change in attitude . . . he said something about praying with that Mr. Moody."

Casey's eyes widened as he remembered Tucker kneeling on the sidewalk by the Bible Institute wagon. He'd thought the big bully was just putting on an act! Could God really change someone like Tucker?

✧ ✧ ✧ ✧

Tucker's apology had a strange effect on Doreen Watkins. A week before, she'd gone to "Moody's show" in the big circus tent out of mere curiosity; this Sunday, Casey realized his mother could hardly wait to hear the man preach.

Casey felt a strange eagerness, too. He hurried through his chores in the elephant quarters as quickly as he could, changed out of his smelly clothes, and slicked his dyed hair with some water. As they tried to find three seats together, Doreen was nervous about the thousands of people filling up the tent. "Help me keep an eye on Cara," she told Casey. "We gotta stick together."

The first hour of Moody's show was similar to last week: an hour of enthusiastic singing—led by the big-voiced Ira Sankey—mixed with solos, "special numbers," choir anthems, and "testimonies."

And then Mr. Moody got up to speak. "My text for today," he boomed from the platform in the center of the tent, "is, 'The Son of Man is come to seek and to save that which was lost.' The question is, my friends, who is lost? Some people think they are saved because they go to church. But I wanna tell you even the devil goes to church. . . . Another class of people think they are saved because they try to live right. Is that salvation? No. All our 'goodness' is like a bunch of filthy rags. . . . Still another group of people thinks they are saved because they always say their prayers. But I tell you, saying your prayers is not the same as being born again. . . ."

Casey was bewildered. Surely people who went to church, tried to live by the Ten Commandments, and said their prayers weren't "lost." But Mr. Moody was standing on that platform saying that *everybody* was lost! It didn't matter, he said, if a person was rich or poor . . . a king or a peasant . . . a person with fancy letters after his name or a coal miner with little education. Only Jesus Christ, the Good Shepherd, could find us and bring us back home.

As Mr. Moody continued telling the story about the Good Shepherd risking His life to hunt for the one lost sheep, Casey noticed tears glistening on his mother's cheeks. He started to think; was he lost, too? He'd sure felt lost when he failed to do the double pass and let everybody down. But now that he'd worked up the courage to go back up on the trapeze, he was starting to feel good about himself again. Was he still lost?

"Cara! Where's Cara?" his mother's voice suddenly hissed into his ear. Startled, Casey looked around. He thought Cara was sitting on the bench right beside his mother. But—she wasn't there!

Doreen Watkins was already pushing her way through the crowd, searching for Cara. Casey went in the opposite direction, but as he scanned the enormous crowd, he knew it would be like looking for a needle in a haystack. Why had his little sister wandered off? Or—

He hardly dared think about the other possiblity. Pickpockets and thieves were always hanging around circus crowds. What if . . . what if someone had grabbed Cara and run off with her?

Chapter 13

...And Found

CASEY SAW HIS MOTHER frantically looking up one row and down the next . . . then he lost sight of her as the entire crowd stood up to sing the final song. Now they would never find little Cara!

Craning his neck this way and that, Casey elbowed his way past men and women singing, "Just as I am, without one plea," not caring whose toes he stepped on.

And then, as he came to an aisle, he saw her . . . being pulled along by Tucker!

"Hey!" Casey shouted. But his voice was swallowed up by the thousands of singing voices all around him. Furious, Casey tried to run along the aisle, dodging people stepping out from their seats and heading for the platform. So! It was Tucker all along! All that business about being a changed man was just an act after all. Maybe he'd done it so they'd let down their guard . . . maybe he'd been planning to steal Cara all along!

Coming to where two aisles crossed, Casey looked up and down. Which direction did they go? Why were all these people in the aisles? Then he saw them in the distance, Cara skipping alongside the brawny man, merging with the throng heading toward the center of the tent. "Hey! Stop that man!" he yelled, running after them. But again, his voice couldn't be heard above the singing.

Casey jostled his way to where he last saw the pair. He'd lost sight of them! His heart seemed to be beating in his throat—he couldn't lose them now! He'd been so close! Running down another aisle, he barely noticed that the singing had stopped and a hush was settling over the crowd . . . and then he heard Mr. Moody's voice booming out over their heads.

"We have a lost child here . . . a lost child . . ."

Jerking his head around, Casey looked toward the platform. There was Tucker handing Cara up to Mr. Moody. The preacher held the little girl in his arms and turned back to the crowd. "Will the mother  of this child come to the platform immediately?"

Fighting his way through the crowd, Casey arrived at the platform at almost the same moment as his mother. Doreen Watkins was sobbing with relief as she held out her arms toward Mr. Moody.

Mr. Moody caught Casey's eye. "Is this your mother and little sister, son?"

Speechless, Casey nodded. Out of the corner of his eye, he saw Tucker standing off to the side, smiling broadly.

Mr. Moody knelt down and lowered Cara into her mother's arms. Then he looked into Doreen Watkins's grateful eyes and said, "This is what Jesus Christ came to do, good sister—to seek and to save lost sinners and restore them to their Heavenly Father's embrace."

Weeping, Doreen said, "Oh, please, sir . . . I want Jesus to find me, too!"

Within moments, one of Mr. Moody's assistants was ushering the three Watkinses into some chairs behind the platform, along with others who had come forward at Moody's invitation. The young man showed them verses in the Bible that talked about God's love, the importance of confessing one's sins, and accepting Jesus as Savior and Lord.

"Oh yes," said Doreen. "I want to do that. Will you pray with me?"

The assistant turned to Casey. "How about you, young man? Do you want to give your life to Jesus, too?"

Casey's mind had been tumbling with everything that had happened this past week . . . and how wrong he'd been about Tucker just now.

"Yes," he said slowly. "Yes, I do." If Mr. Moody's

God loved someone like Tucker and could turn *his* life around, then he wanted to know Him, too.

"Me, too," said Cara shyly.

A few minutes later, as the little family of three finished praying, Casey saw Mr. Moody coming toward them.

"Oh, Mr. Moody," said Doreen, "could I please talk to you? I . . . I have lost my husband and need some advice."

"Of course, my good woman," Mr. Moody said, lowering his stout frame into a chair and winking at Cara.

"I joined the circus this year," Doreen went on, "because I thought it would be the answer to some of our problems." She briefly sketched what had happened between Jack Watkins's death and her decision to join Forepaugh's Circus. "But . . . it's not really the life I want for myself and my children. In fact, I would leave today, but Chicago is a foreign place to me. Where would I go? What would I do?"

"Hmm." Mr. Moody stroked his whiskers and looked sideways at Casey. "This young man was asking those same questions a few days ago." Casey reddened. "How long is your contract with the circus, Mrs. Watkins?"

"Until the end of this season—four more months."

"Then," Moody said, "unless you are asked to do something against your conscience, I advise you to finish out your contract. I don't want it said that D. L. Moody encouraged someone to break an agreement."

"But . . . what about my children's schooling?" Casey's mother asked.

Mr. Moody didn't answer. Instead he turned to Casey and asked, "Did you go back up on that trapeze."

Casey nodded. "Yes, sir . . . five days now. But with a simpler act."

Mr. Moody threw back his head and laughed. "Good for you, son! Mrs. Watkins, if you still want to leave the circus at the end of this season, write me here." He scribbled an address in Northfield, Massachusetts, on a scrap of paper. "I have started two secondary schools there for young people Casey's age—one for boys, one for girls. If you want the boy to finish his education, I will help him get a scholarship to Mount Hermon Boys School."

Mr. Moody turned back to Casey with a big grin. "And when you finish secondary school, young man, if you're still interested in becoming one of D. L. Moody's gap-men . . . *then* we'll talk about you coming here to the Chicago Bible Institute!"

❖ ❖ ❖ ❖

The three Watkinses changed into their costumes for the Sunday afternoon two o'clock performance in a kind of happy daze. It was the same routine they'd been doing twice a day for six weeks . . . but somehow, everything seemed different.

After intermission, as Casey waited with the Eugene brothers at the performers' entrance for the ringmaster to announce their act, Pierre Eugene asked casually, "So, Watkins, what do you think about doing the double pass today?"

Casey blinked. He hadn't even been thinking about it.

Pierre shrugged. "It's your call."

To his surprise, Casey realized it didn't really matter. He thought he could do it—no, he *knew* he could do it—but he didn't *have* to do it to prove anything to anybody, even himself. God loved him . . . with or without the trapeze act.

"Sure," he shrugged back and grinned. "Why not?"

So, with no fanfare at all to the sparse Sunday afternoon crowd, the "Eugene Twins" hurtled through the air past each other . . . and Casey felt Pierre's firm grip on his wrists as Ansel caught the

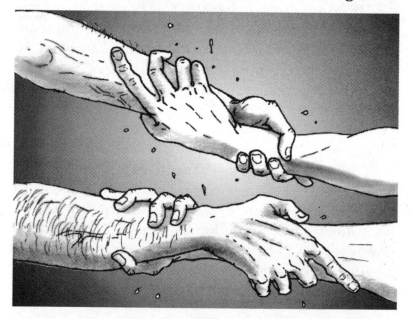

fly bar Casey had just left.

A startled ringmaster sputtered, "Did you see that, ladies and gentlemen? A spectacular double pass!" As the four "brothers" rolled off the net, bowed to the delighted crowd, and ran out of the tent, Casey felt a warm glow start deep inside and spill out on his face.

He'd finally done the double pass . . . in front of a crowd.

Suddenly Casey felt himself being grabbed up in a big bear hug by Eph Thompson. "You did it, Casey Watkins!" the man yelled. "I knew you could! I always knew it!" He put Casey down and laughed. "But it wouldn't have helped for me to tell you. You had to tell yourself."

✧ ✧ ✧ ✧

The last performance of the season was given at Forepaugh's winter quarters in Philadelphia. Afterward everyone from clowns to roustabouts clustered noisily around Joe McCaddon to receive their last paycheck.

The circus manager climbed up on a wooden box and held up his hands for silence. "I got an announcement ta make," he growled, sending a puff of cigar smoke spiraling upward. "Frankly, in spite of the Chicago World's Fair booking, total box office receipts for the season hit an all-time low—for the second year in a row."

Performers and crew shifted nervously. They

knew what was coming.

McCaddon raised his voice. "After consulting with the owner, James Bailey, a decision has been reached to cut the size of Forepaugh's Circus in half."

Groans and angry mutterings erupted from the assembled crew. "Bailey should fire McCaddon first," someone muttered behind Casey.

"Can't," someone else snorted. "McCaddon is Bailey's brother-in-law."

"Shh!" Casey said. "He's gonna read the list."

Acts that were being retained included Addie Forepaugh, Jr., liberty horse, elephant, and wild animal acts . . . Lillie Deacon, bareback riding . . . Ella Zuila, bicycle highwire act . . . The Eugene Brothers', trapeze act . . .

McCaddon continued reading the list for several minutes. But Casey was mainly aware of the names that *weren't* read. Neither Doreen Watkins nor Eph Thompson's name were on the list.

"*Doreen! Casey! Cara!*" a woman's voice squealed.

Startled, Casey turned around. There was something familiar about that voice . . . and then he saw them: Aunt Mary, Uncle John, and cousin Elspeth awkwardly pushing through the crowd toward them.

"Why, Mary . . . and John!" Doreen Watkins said. "What in the world are you doing here?"

"Well, I told John we owed it to his brother Jack to come see his family perform in the circus," Mary Watkins gushed, hugging Doreen and each of the children in turn. "You were simply marvelous, Doreen . . . wasn't she, John?"

"Uh, yes . . . yes," the Rev. John Watkins said, clearly uncomfortable being surrounded by men and women in sequins and tights and gaily colored plumes. "Quite remarkable."

"But you were the best, cousin Casey," said Elspeth, her eyes shining with admiration. "I couldn't believe it was really you up there on that flying trapeze!"

"Oh my, yes," said Aunt Mary proudly. "Amazing. Absolutely amazing."

"Harumph!" coughed Uncle John. "Yes, yes, Mary's right. You were all very good. Looks, uh . . . like you've found your calling," John Watkins admitted.

Doreen Watkins gave a short laugh. "Hardly. The circus is being cut in half. We've been sacked."

"You've been—oh!" exclaimed Casey's aunt. "Why, then . . . John?" Mary Watkins gave her husband a "Say something!" look.

Uncle John seemed relieved. "Well, now, if that's the case, maybe we can let bygones be bygones. If you're ready to settle down, Doreen, maybe we can find some work for you here in Philadelphia—"

"You *must* come stay with us until you get settled!" Mary Watkins insisted.

Feeling desperate at the way things were going, Casey poked his mother. Doreen Watkins smiled politely. "You're both very kind. I'll . . . think about it."

Rev. Watkins looked offended. "You'll *think* about it? Why, we've just offered to—"

"Casey!" Pierre Eugene, followed closely by Raoul

137

and Ansel, came striding over to the little group. Elspeth stared, fascinated, at the muscular French brothers in their bright costumes that matched the one Casey was wearing. "The Eugene Brothers act is being kept on with the circus!" Pierre said eagerly, then he noticed the family group. "Oh . . . sorry, Mrs. Watkins. We heard you've been cut. But . . . that doesn't mean Casey has been cut. He's part of our act, now. He could travel with us."

Casey was startled. He hadn't thought of that. And, he had to admit, once he'd gotten over the panic of performing in front of crowds, he'd really enjoyed being part of The Eugene Brothers' act the last few months.

On the other hand, how long would it last? The circus had been losing money for two years and was being cut in half. What if the Eugenes got sacked next year and returned to France . . . what would he do then? He was fifteen now, and already behind in school . . .

Casey realized everyone was staring at him, waiting for him to say something. His eyes met his mother's, and he remembered: Mr. Moody's offer.

He squared his shoulders. "Thank you, Pierre. But I'm not really a Eugene. I'm a Watkins and my place is with my family right now. Besides, I'm going to school!"

✧ ✧ ✧ ✧

After a long talk with her children in the circus

railroad car that night, Doreen Watkins pulled out a sheet of writing paper.

"Dear Mr. Moody," she began writing. "You said to write you when the circus season was over. It's over in more ways than one: my contract has not been renewed. So it is working out for the best.

"I'm writing about the Mount Hermon Boys School you mentioned for Casey. I would very much like for him to get a Christian education. I have no money, but I am willing to work for his tuition. Do you think your schools might have a job for me? I am a very good seamstress and could cook and sew for your girls school across the river. Then when Cara is old enough, maybe she could go to the girls school, as well. . . ."

More About Dwight L. Moody

DWIGHT LYMAN MOODY, born February 5, 1837, in Northfield, Massachusetts, was only four years old when his father, a brick mason, died. Left with nine children under the age of thirteen, Betsey Moody had her hands full just keeping her large brood clothed and fed. As a result, Dwight's total schooling probably equaled a fifth-grade education today.

Young Dwight's greatest ambition was to get away from tiny Northfield and get rich. He left home at age seventeen and went to work for his uncle in Boston as a shoe salesman. But his uncle required Dwight to go to Sunday school, where the teacher challenged the eager young man to trust Christ for forgiveness of sin, leading to Dwight's conversion.

Dwight liked selling shoes. He had a natural gift

of salesmanship. But Boston was too stuffy for him; in 1856 the twenty-year-old headed west to Chicago where he landed a job with C. E. Wisall, the shoe tycoon. Now his ambition was to save $100,000. Within a few years Dwight was traveling around the Midwest representing Wisell's shoes—but he always made it back to Chicago on Sunday to pick up kids for the mission Sunday school he'd helped organize, which eventually numbered over a thousand.

One of the Sunday school workers, Emma Revell, attracted Moody's attention. He announced his engagement to the sixteen-year-old Emma by simply stating that he was "no longer available to escort the other young ladies home"!

Young Moody, aware of his lack of education and biblical knowledge, did not feel qualified to be a teacher, but when asked to assist with home visitation, Moody reluctantly accompanied a sickly teacher named Mr. Hibbert who wanted to win each girl in his class to Christ before he died. The experience of the conversion of these "slum girls" to Christ so profoundly affected Moody that he quit the shoe business altogether for "full time Christian service."

The Young Man's Christian Association (YMCA) appointed Moody as a missionary. During the Civil war, he served as a YMCA chaplain to soldiers stationed near Chicago. (Moody did not enlist as a soldier because he felt it would be wrong to take the life of another human being.) During the war, he married Emma Revell (then twenty), and two years later they welcomed a daughter, also named Emma.

During the next few years the energetic and innovative Dwight Moody helped his mission Sunday school grow into the Illinois Street Independent Church, enrolled as a seminary student, and was elected president of the Chicago YMCA.

Because his humble beginnings emphasized thrift, hard work, and close family ties, Moody maintained a good rapport with common folks and always had a genuine compassion for the poor. But he also became well-known among wealthy evangelicals, who supported his ministries.

In 1867, Moody spent four months visiting and speaking at YMCAs in Great Britain. While in England he met two giants of the faith, Charles Spurgeon and George Müller. He also met Rev. Henry Varley, who challenged Moody with these words: "The world has yet to see what God can do with one man wholly dedicated to Him." These words so inspired Moody that he vowed to become that man.

In 1870, at a YMCA International Convention, he heard a hymn singer with an impressive voice. He invited Ira Sankey to join him as music director; for the next two decades "Moody and Sankey" became linked as a world-famous evangelistic team.

On October 8, 1871, the Great Chicago Fire destroyed Moody's new home, the YMCA Farwell Hall Moody had helped build, *and* the Illinois Street Church. At first shaken, Moody soon saw the leveling of his organizational work in Chicago as an opportunity to plunge more fully into evangelistic work.

The era of the great evangelistic campaigns was

launched, beginning with two years in Great Britain (England, Scotland, and Ireland). Subsequent campaigns took him back to Great Britain (a total of seven times), to New England, Mexico, Canada, the western United States, Europe, and the Holy Land—right up to the time of his death at the end of the century.

In 1876 he purchased a farm in Northfield, Massachusetts, where his mother was still living. Here he spent the summer months, enjoying his children, and later his grandchildren. Even though Moody had little education himself, he established two schools in the area, Northfield Seminary for Girls and Mount Hermon School for Boys.

Meanwhile back in Chicago, a woman named Emiline Dryer had a vision for a Bible school for laypeople; she wanted Moody's organizational and fundraising skills to make it a reality. The Chicago Bible Institute formally opened in 1889; only after Moody's death was it renamed the Moody Bible Institute.

Moody was also instrumental in establishing two publishing houses, Fleming H. Revell (named after Emma's brother, who published many of Moody's sermons), and the Bible Institute Colportage Association (later renamed Moody Press).

In 1892, while returning to the United States with his son Will on the ocean liner *Spree*, a near-fatal accident at sea caused Moody to redouble his evangelistic efforts—even though his doctor had told him to slow down. Time was short! People were lost! Only work done for Christ was important. This led to a major campaign during the Chicago World's Fair the following year—a six-month evangelistic effort that included renting Adam Forepaugh's Circus tent. His youngest son, Paul, only fifteen at the time, was with him during this campaign.

Moody the man was a bundle of seeming contradictions. Uneducated himself, he established three schools. He preached to thousands around the world, but was remembered by his children as a devoted father. He rubbed shoulders with statesmen, but had a special heart for young people—and horses. He loved to play practical jokes; at home he wore "disreputable clothes" and drove his horse and buggy at breakneck speeds around his Northfield farm. As one of his sons remarked, he was "a stout and bearded Peter Pan, a boy who never really grew up."

Just before the turn of the century, his weak heart forced him to cut an evangelistic trip short. Only sixty-two, he died December 22, 1899, at his home in Northfield, where he is buried.

For Further Reading:

Bailey, Faith Coxe. *D. L. Moody—The Valley and the World.* Chicago: Moody Press, 1959. For youth.

Curtis, Richard K. *They Called Him Mister Moody.* Garden City, N.Y.: Doubleday & Co., 1962. For youth.

Moody, William R. *D. L. Moody.* New York: The MacMillan Company, 1930. A second biography by his oldest son, more accurate than the original (1900).

Moody, Paul. *My Father: An Intimate Portrait of Dwight L. Moody.* Boston: Little, Brown, 1938. Not a biography, Moody's youngest son tells many delightful stories; a behind-the-scenes portrait.